DISGRACED

Rosemary Ling

Clarke Books
Anna María, Florida

Also by Rosemary Ling (with Barbara Kingsmore)
Maddie's Paradise Mountain
I Remember Grandma: A Love Legacy

Claᴙke Books
Anna Maᴙía, Floᴙíɒa

Published by Clarke Books/Anna Maria Island, Florida
Copyright © 2011 by Rosemary Ling
All rights reserved. Published by Clarke Books

Cover & Interior book design by:
Noire Creative Concepts
www.noirecreative.com

Printed in the U.S.A.
First printed April 2011

Also available in electronic formats for:
Amazon Kindle
Barnes & Noble Nook
Sony E-Reader

visit the publisher's website at:
www.clarkebooks.net

dedication

It takes many beautiful flowers to make a garden. It takes many beautiful friends to read, encourage and help with putting together a special book such as this. To all those friends who assisted on this project I thank you with all my heart. I especially would like to mention Eunice Kuykendall whose time, patience, and good advice helped me enormously in this endeavor. Most of all this work is dedicated to the woman who is my mother. No matter what she had to endure, in her life, I always knew that I was loved.

author's introduction

You could look at this title Disgraced and wonder about the strangeness of this story. You might think that it wouldn't be your cup of tea. "How could a person sink so low?" You might ask yourself "How could a woman live on the streets, drink booze and even sell herself to men for money." How ashamed this woman would be to look you in the eye and tell you this story. She was so sorry to have been such a 'bad woman.' This book is a small glimpse into her tragic life.

Maybe your life has been what most people would call normal, at least on the outside with mothers, fathers, brothers, sisters and school friends. You might be a person who would have a hard time understanding a different kind of life in which sin and shame had changed people. Way back in the 1920s many people lived a life of poverty in the coal mining towns of West Virginia. It wasn't strange for two or three sisters to share one small bed. There was no indoor plumbing or running water.

Try to imagine a frog in a well as he jumps up three

feet only to slide down two feet. I know you probably are thinking people who live in this manner bring hardship on themselves. It is their own fault because they did all the wrong things. Well...you would be correct and the woman in this story would agree with you. She never made excuses or blamed anyone but herself.

It was a time when work in West Virginia was scarce and money was very hard to come by. This story will take you into the depths of one woman's hell — a life filled with hopelessness, disappointment and despair. A secret is revealed that spirals her life out of control--making one bad choice after another. However, Margaret learns that just like God can turn an ugly caterpillar into a beautiful butterfly, He can change her life because He is in control. No matter how bad the circumstances may seem there is always hope when He is by your side.

1
a coal mining town
in west virginia

I heard the screaming from the next bedroom. The awful sound seemed to go on forever. All of us children were huddled together in the back bedroom. I was the oldest girl in the family. We put our hands over our ears to stop the awful sound. The others clung to me. One of the little boys had wet his pants because of so much fear. The screaming suddenly stopped and then we heard the sound of a baby cry! Mother had just given birth to her ninth child in the front bedroom. What a relief we all felt at that moment. Then we all clapped our hands because we were very glad that this time of waiting was finally over. The old country doctor had arrived just in time to help with the birth of our new baby brother. I was twelve and that made me the oldest girl in the family. I felt that I was very mature or grown up for my age. I would tell myself that my parents needed my help around the house, especially at such important times as these. It, in some ways, made me act proud. Almost as if I was a know-it-all and...a little bossy. My mother was so busy each time, after she had a baby, she would hand our new brother or sister over to me. I told all of the other children to stay in the backroom and be very quiet. I needed to go in and see about our mother and to help out with the new baby. The doctor had already left our home by then. Women in those days were made to stay in bed for ten whole days after giving birth. So I would be the main care giver while Dad was at work in the coal mines. I could however, call in a neighbor lady if I had a problem that was too much for me. Girls seemed to grow up very fast back in those days, learning to cook meals and care for little children and newborn babies.

I opened the door slowly and walked into my parent's bedroom and I could see that Mother and her new baby were both sound asleep. Looking around the room, I first noticed the old oak dresser drawer standing in the far corner. It had been made by mother's father fifty years ago. He liked to work with wood and lovingly built all of the bedroom furniture piece by piece with a hand saw. All of this furniture had been used first by his family and then passed down to our family later, when it was no longer needed by them. Grandpa had also built the old rocker that mother had nursed all of the babies from. It had no arms on the sides and was placed next to her bed. There were also two smaller beds where some of the younger children could sleep at times. Just to be near mother and daddy or if perhaps one became ill.

Looking closer, I saw the oak night stand by the side of the bed that had been a wedding gift for my parents. Her old family Bible was still opened to the Psalms and a page was marked with a white hand-crocheted cross. There were hand embroidered dresser scarves on both the night stand and the dresser that had been handed down from Grandma Weaver on my daddy's side.

I always felt extra special coming into mother and daddy's room because it was the same bed I had been born in long ago. It was so soft and warm and still very comforting to me. The beautiful quilt that was covering the bed was baby blue with little white daisy flowers on it. Mom and I had worked for three whole months, in the evenings last year, quilting and making it. Stitch by stitch we had quilted each piece.

The headboard also matched the oak dresser that grandpa had made. White lace curtains were yellowed with age but still covered the two bedroom windows. There was a dim light coming from an old metal floor lamp standing tall beside the bed and rocking chair. As I glanced around the room once again, I remembered that last spring I had helped to put up the wallpaper. The blue in the paper matched the blue in the quilt. To me it was all worth the time and effort that we had put into it. All of the little children seemed to be happy, as they watched mother and I work together on projects that made our home look nicer.

Looking closely at my mother, I noticed how tired she looked. She was thirty five years old now but she looked much older because of having so many children and too much work which took its toll on a person back then. She smiled at me, as she opened her eyes and saw me coming toward her. She depended on me so much and knew that I would take good care of her and the new baby until my dad came home from work. I felt that I was very mature for my age and I really did enjoy being the oldest girl. My brother Russell is older than I, though he could not do woman's work like me. He had his own chores to do around our house, bringing coal and water for cooking, as well as working in the garden during the summer months.

I went outside to the old cistern next to the back porch and got a pail of water and heated it on the old, coal stove. Then I poured the warm water into the basin on the kitchen table. I then carefully spread out a small, yellow flannel, receiving blanket and laid out a washcloth and towel to wrap the baby in after his bath. I picked out a soft white flannel nightgown from the package of baby clothes inside mother's dresser drawer. During the long months of her pregnancy mother and I had made some clothes for our new baby as we awaited the newest arrival. Each baby was special to us. Like a gift from God, which our parents had said many times to us. We were poor in material things but we were loved very much.

I went back into the bedroom to get the newborn baby boy. I picked him up and touched his little fuzzy head of blond hair. Then I bathed him in the warm water with a small piece of Ivory soap. After dressing him in his little night gown, I held him close to me and breathed in the smell of a new baby. In my heart there would always be room for one more little one. This had been a long hard labor and birth. I had heard my mother cry in agony for many long hours before the baby had finally been born. I sighed with much relief, as I took him in and laid my sweet little baby brother in my mother's arms. Looking through the bedroom window I could see that the sunshine was almost gone from the day as the light was fading and night was closing in. Daddy would be home soon from the coal mine. I always felt relief to hear the sound of his footsteps coming through the door. When he arrived home from the mines late that night he was beaming with joy and seemed so happy, especially when I told him that the baby had already been born and everything had turned out fine. Looking closely at my Dad, I noticed that his hair was getting grey at the temples, when he combed it back after washing up from work. He knew that all of the coal dust had to be cleaned off before coming near mom and the baby. He then went into see mom as she was nursing the baby. Such peace seemed to fill that room. I quietly stood near the door way and watched each one, especially my dad.

He seemed always to have so much love for his family. He said " It was one more mouth to feed, but it was one more to love." He gently kissed mom on the cheek and bent over to whisper something softly in her ear. Mother smiled and looked up at Daddy and said, "How about if we named him Lucas? " He gently laid his huge hands on the baby's tiny head and big tears welled up in his eyes. Then he said "that would be a nice name for our new son. Are you doing alright?" Mother smiled and said "I will be fine my dear just a little tired. I am so glad that you are home with us and safe and sound from the coal mines. Please try and get some rest yourself you must be tired too."

Then daddy turned to me and stretched out his big arms. I went right to him and he held me tightly for a time and said to me "I can always count on my big girl." Daddies hugs always made me feel special. My Dad was only thirty-seven years old but working in the coal mines six days a week, twelve hours a day, also made him appear much older. They hardly had enough money coming in to keep a roof over our heads, clothes on our backs and enough food on the table but at times such as these I was so very proud to be apart of this wonderful family!

I had prepared plenty of food earlier in the day for our supper. A large pot of pinto beans and corn bread would feed all of us a good meal tonight. After feeding them and then tucking all of the little ones into bed for the night I felt that a good job was completed for today. Mother and dad were in bed,the whole house became quiet and peaceful so now at last I could rest my weary bones.

2

one day in my world

It was the early 1900s, and the war was on everyone's mind. It was such a cold and gray day my breath turned white when I exhaled. The sulfur smell from the coal mines hung in the air and never seemed to dissipate. A light snow had fallen overnight covering the normally blacken soot-covered ground. As the wind blew in little gusts, the white would give way to the ever present layer of ebony powder that seemed to be everywhere.

The early days of April, that year, brought hope that spring would soon be here. Spring meant planting gardens and gardens meant fresh vegetables, a welcomed change from the dried pinto beans consumed by so many over the long winter months. It was not uncommon to have eaten the brown beans twice a day for weeks at a time. Cornbread, made from ground corn meal baked in a blacken skillet was a warm welcomed treat when served with the pinto beans. Biscuits and flour gravy served for breakfast offered the only variation. Eggs were scarce and those who could afford it would enjoy slab bacon purchased from the company owned store. Occasionally a hog was killed and pork was shared. This was salty and fatty; yielding a great deal of grease which was used for flavor.

Twelve year old Margaret Weaver loved walking the foot hills of Paint Creek Hollow in Burnwell, West Virginia. The Blue Ridge Mountains provided a perfect canvass of fall colors before the cold fingers, of winter hands, wrapped around these unspoiled mountains. However, today, as twelve year old Margaret looked around, it was as if all of the color had been removed, and the world seemed to exist in black and white with various shades of gray. This was the result of many years of men burrowing deep into the black earth to reach rich deposits of coal which seemed to be in unlimited supply all over the region. Once removed, sifted and loaded onto trains, the black power clung to every surface. Hours of cleaning would only yield temporary relief from the filthy soot, only to have it settle once again within a few hours.

Only a few short years ago this region was uninhabited. Great bears and many different kinds of wildlife were plentiful for the mountaineers who lived and raised their families here. Margaret, along with her mother, father and eight siblings, lived in a gray weathered shack at the base of Paint Creek Hollow. Margaret often hiked up the hollow, to a clearing that overlooked the beautiful green, rolling hills of Kanawha County, to watch magnificent orange, pink and purple sunsets atop the majestic Blue Ridge Mountains. However, this area, once green and pure was now terminally blackened by coal dust.

It was no secret that Margaret's love for the mountains reached far beyond its beauty and solitude. The mountains were magical and inspiring and helped her to connect to her family's roots. A journey along the dirt roads to the top meant revisiting her grandparent's past. Margaret's grandpa Weaver had built the one room shanty over fifty years ago on the very top of the mountain. It was there where he lived with his dear wife, Rebecca until turning ninety-two.

The hilltop where the shanty stood had spectacular views of yellow and violet wild flowers that took her breath away and garnet sumac bushes dotted the landscape. It had at times seemed to her as if God had taken a paint brush and splashed vibrant colors all across the whole world, as far as eye could see. Margaret loved to smell the lilacs that were so fragrant as well as the sweet honeysuckle that grew along the old country fence bordering the side of the shanty. The smell of the lilacs and honeysuckle captivated her senses in spring and summer as she approached the old shanty. She remembered her grandmother Weaver gathering bouquets of lilacs for the kitchen table and how wonderful they made the whole house smell. On the front of the old, wooden, tar-papered shanty there was a small wrap around porch with broken slats. As Margaret stepped onto the dilapidated porch, she moved slowly and deliberately across the front entrance to avoid injury. As she slowly swung open the old wooden door, she found the living room empty and musty from yesterday's rain. However, the quietness and charm was warm and inviting, even though it had not been lived in since grandpa's death from a heart-attack two years ago. A ladder led up to a loft where the one bedroom was located. A feather-bed filled most of the small space and had been damaged by mice. There were mice droppings on the floor which led to a large mouse nest in the old coal stove. On this day the birds seemed to be more special as their songs carried on the wind.

Outside, red cardinals, blue jays and finches sang and honey bees swarmed in their combs along the roof's edge. Deer came to feed on berries at the back of the property.

Margaret sat quietly on the porch step enjoying the young fawns frolicking in the tall grasses.

The mountains were indescribably beautiful and it was at her favorite time of the day. Early one morning, as the sun began to rise, Margaret ascended to the mountain top. She needed to get away from all of the pressures of her home life. It was one place where Margaret felt close to God. It was here where she came to dream and to escape the harsh realities of her current life. Her parents had allowed Margaret this freedom after her chores had been completed. In the still darkness of early morn, many hours before the rising of the sun to greet the new day. This was a special privilege given to her at times. Her big brother Russell would be around some time later in the morning to make sure that she was safe and he to had also enjoyed the mountain trips. When his chores were completed, many times he could be heard whistling a tune as he climbed the mountain path up to the old shanty.

3
remembering back

Many times when Margaret would closed her eyes, she could still see herself as a very little girl. When she was the only little girl in the family. She so loved being close by her Mama in bed. When her Daddy went to work early in the mornings, Margaret would quietly slip into their room and lie down with her mama. How she would enjoy just laying there together, the two of them alone. Her mother would sometimes cuddle her for a long time, calling her by her pet name "Angel." Margaret recalled the times when her Mama would brush her hair and put it into two braids with little ribbons on the ends. She was such a happy child back then. She really liked her brother Russell, who was a big boy three years older than Margaret. She remembered daddy would sometimes lift her high up over his head and kissing her on both cheeks. Margaret loved to sing the songs that she heard her mother singing, as she worked in the kitchen preparing meals. She taught Margaret to peel potatoes and carrots. She enjoyed helping her mother in the kitchen and helped her to wash dishes and dry the pots and pans. Life was so good then for Margaret. After a time mother began throwing up after breakfast and Margaret worried, asking what is wrong? *Nothing is wrong dear!* She was told not to be concerned. She watched mother and daddy look at one another with a loving smile, as if they had a secret but she wished someone would tell it to her.

Then Margaret began to see a change in her mothers shape, she was getting a very big belly. "What's wrong?" she would ask of her Mother. Her Mother finally replied, "You are going to get a new baby sister or brother." She remembered telling her Mother in tears, "Why, I like being your "Angel", we don't need anyone else." Mother explained to Margaret, "you are a big girl now and it will be nice to have another little one. You can help me to take care of him, or her and help teach the baby many new things. When the baby's old enough you can teach it to sing all of our songs and play outside in the warm sunshine. You will be the big sister."

As the months passed Margaret tried to be happy about the baby coming. Then one night she was awakened by her Mother crying and Margaret ran to her bedroom to see what was wrong. Daddy put Margaret back in her bed saying that the doctor was with Mother and that the new baby was going to be born. Margaret listened intently from her bed when she heard a long scream from her Mother, then she heard a baby cry. Margaret was so frightened that she began to cry and felt so alone. Just then Margaret's older brother Russell came into her bedroom to hold her and told her not to cry that everything was going to be all right. Russell stayed with Margaret for about an hour holding her hand, then Daddy came into Margaret's bedroom and took both Margaret and Russell in to see their Mother. She lay propped up in bed on two pillows with her long hair was lying around her face like a halo. Her cheeks were rosy and she had tears in her eyes, that seemed to sparkle with joy. She looked so pretty to Margaret and Margaret thought she truly was a vision. Mother smiled and reached out to her saying, "Come in my sweet children, come and see your new little sister." The baby was red faced and wrinkled, she was crying loudly with her little fist waving in the air. She was wrapped in a pink blanket and looked so tiny lying there in my Mother's arms. Daddy said, "Isn't she beautiful." With that Margaret started to sob again loudly and ran back in to her own bedroom. She knew that things in her young life were going to change with a new baby and that her life would never be the same again. Someone else had taken her place, her special, warm place. The baby was named, Macel and she will be my Mother's baby now and Margaret was to be the big sister. Margaret grew very quiet, not talking or singing much in the next few weeks. Then one morning Mother lay down with Margaret on her bed. She said, "My sweet "Angel", you were sent to me from God, you will always be my own little daughter, I love you and no one could ever take your place. The baby, Macel is a gift to you and she will bless your life if you allow her to. You can help care for her and share our family together and we can all find joy. No one will ever be my special 'Angel' but you." As she wiped away the tears with her hand she felt so much better. She knew deep down within her heart that she was her Mother's favorite child.

This then began a new pattern of a very busy family life for Margaret when every few years another baby arrived. As she grew older Margaret became a second mother to first, Macel and then Maxine and all the other siblings that came later. She was like a little mother to all of these needy children of various ages. Like little duck-lings they would follow Margaret around from the time they could crawl or walk. Margaret was the one they came to for their shoes and sox to be put on, or to feed them their meals. Margaret remembered when she always had one or two of them sleeping with her in her bed. At times Margaret would close her eyes and remember the special times when life was simple and their home was quiet and mother could have time for only her. To read Margaret a bedtime story or tell her about her childhood days. Life was so good back then, before all the babies came and Margaret became their second Mom. Now she had learned to accept that way that life was to be and she found a certain pleasure in knowing that she was loved and needed.

Then, came the first day of school, the turning point in life for Margaret. School was fun and scary and strange all rolled up into one big day. Her teacher, Miss Grayson, was an old, grey-haired woman who didn't smile much. Daddy said that the teacher had to be stern so that all the children would listen and be serious and quiet. However, Margaret would always recall the second day of school. She was out in the schoolyard and tripped over a big rock falling down and skinning her knee. This nice boy came over to her and helped her and the teacher get the sore knee cleaned up and bandaged. His name was Howard Jones and she learned later that he was two years older than her. From the very first day that he sat next to her, in the class room, she liked him. He was very quiet-mannered and he seemed to study hard. It was his great big, brown eyes that first drew Margaret to him. She found out that his family was new in the town. However, they would also be going to the same church as her. Margaret and Howard were just two young kids in years but in her heart she had already picked him out to some-day be her husband. Little did she know of the future and what was to come?

Year after year Margaret and Howard became closer, without many words ever being spoken between them. Margaret's whole family attended the little Baptist church every Sunday and so did Howard's family. Margaret would gaze across the room at times and she would catch Howard looking back at her and her young heart would skip a beat. You can guess that her mind was not on what the preacher was talking about but on Howard Jones instead. Margaret tried to be a good student and pay close attention in school. She did enjoy reading and hearing stories about American history. Especially about her ancestors who had migrated here to West Virginia. She found that at a very young age she had a knack for writing children's stories and she enjoyed spelling bees, which were so much fun for her to do. In the back of her mind, she always had thoughts about that boy named Howard.

She remembered one day he had given her a Mason Jar filled with some dry grass and some fireflies among it. She loved to watch the little bugs light up. These were a symbol of her joy and made all of the other children laugh as well. She knew that Howard must have felt a very strong attraction to her, to have given her such a special present. In the meantime, Margaret was growing like a weed and getting taller every week. Mother said her dresses were getting much too short for her to wear. Mother had been teaching Margaret how to sew on her old pedal sewing machine. It was a *Singer* and it was Mother's pride and joy. Grandma Bosher had given it to us for Christmas one year. Margaret's mother let her pick the prettiest flour sack for a new dress. It was baby blue in color and Daddy had said that it matched her eyes. Margaret had a new blue ribbon for her hair to match her new dress. She had plans to get all dressed up special for church on the next Sunday. Margaret also wore a lot of her Mom's hand-me-downs, as she grew into them and then she in turn passed them on to her younger sisters. Some of the clothes needed to be altered to fit each one but they kept everyone dressed as best they could.

The boys wore shirts and pants remade and sewn from Daddy's old clothes and hand-me-downs. Times were hard and there was never enough money to buy many things from the company store. Looking back Margaret realized that they were very poor but she never knew it at the time. She was thankful that they had good food on the table and their home was warm and they had plenty of love to go around for everyone. The years seemed to pass by quickly and it's a good thing that they didn't know the future. Margaret was a happy girl until that fateful day when she was forced to quit school to stay at home. Howard also had to quit school to go to work in the coal mines. She felt like her life was going to end as. Margaret loved going to school and learning. More than that she loved Howard Jones and seeing him each day. She didn't know how she could bear not seeing him any more at school. It is said that when life knocks you down, you have two choices: to cry all the time about it or be grown up and make the best of things. Crying is what Margaret chose.

Margaret remembered the long talk that mother had with her about life. She told Margaret about how much she was needed at home and that in a few years she would be all grown up and someday have a family of her own. She said we could choose to be happy or sad with what life brings to us. Daddy was going to have to have a very stern talk with Margaret if she did not quit crying and help her Mother out with all of the cooking. Margaret decided that since no one understood all of her many feelings, about growing up and her secret love for Howard also about leaving school. She would begin writing in a journal that she had received from her Grandmother Bosher on her last birthday. Pouring out her feelings on paper brought some sweet relief from the sadness. Margaret would write in the journal almost every night after all of the work around the house was done. Her diary became her best friend and confidante. When she was not busy being "mother" to all the "little ones" she was learning to cook most of the meals, as her Mom was busy having one baby after another. Mom always looked so worn-out that Margaret promised herself when she and Howard got married she somehow would only have one baby, not a whole house full like her mom. Margaret dreamed of Howard most every night and of having a beautiful home far away and climbing to the top of a mountain to watch the sunsets with him. Maybe even get to see the ocean someday. Every dream she had included Howard and she knew he was to be her one and only "Prince Charming". Church now became the one place where Margaret could catch a glimpse of Howard, now that he was working in the coal mines and they were both out of school. She thought to herself as she watched him across the aisle, "He is so handsome"although he had also looked very tired.

4
family life

Margaret was the eldest girl of eleven children. There was a baby born almost every two years. Margaret was the care giver whenever a new baby arrived. She had four sisters Madge, Maxine, Myrtle and Macel. She also had six brothers Russell, the twins William and Kenneth, Gene, Willis and Lucas.

Everyone had chores to do, including the little ones. They would stand on a chair and dry the dishes or iron clothes. The boys chopped wood and loaded coal into buckets. Some of the children helped in the garden or helped can food in the fall after picking berries for jelly or jams. The children also enjoyed picking apples from the trees bordering the creek. That meant apple pies and because sugar was very scarce, sweets were a real treat.

Margaret had just been out of school for a month after finishing the eighth grade. Margaret's dad made her quit school because he felt the eighth grade was all any girl needed and she had work to do at home. Margaret really liked school but her dad had already made his decision.

and his word was the law in the Weaver household.

The company-owned houses that the miners lived in were two-story frame white house that had turned gray from the soot in the air. All the houses looked alike--that is if you could call them houses. They were more like shacks with three bedrooms, one large living room and a small kitchen. The living room was used for everything such as sewing, reading stories, playing games and just being together. Three girls slept in one room in the same bed and all the boys slept in another room. The youngest two slept in mother and daddy's room in a small crib.

Since the house had no indoor plumbing or running water, they would catch rain water from the roof in large barrels. Rain water was soft and used to wash clothes and to bathe your body. There was a cistern just outside the back of the house next to the kitchen door. The house had no paint on the outside wooden boards. The yard had no grass — just dirt and weeds. At times the little ones would sweep the dirt in the summer months to try to make the yard look prettier. There was no beauty in a coal mining town.

Almost everyone had to grow a vegetable garden to have any thing but beans to eat. When the frost was still on the ground, Margaret's dad, her brother, and some-times her mother would have to help break up the hard frozen earth using an ax shovel or any other tool they could find to work the soil. This would mostly take place in early March. Even after most of winter had passed, the cold wind still blew. Everyone looked forward to spring and warmer temperatures. The garden was the family's only hope for surviving the next winter. Families looked forward to the rows of green beans, yellow squash and cabbage for coleslaw. Other favorites were the fresh ripe tomatoes and corn on the cob. The tomatoes were used in making meatloaf, vegetable soup and tomato pudding.

Seeds were saved from one year to the next and planted in rows in the back yard garden.

All the children would go berry picking to bring home blackberries for jam. It was a joy to fill their pails and take their treasurers home. The children always had to be on the alert, however, for snakes as they sometimes hid under the berry bushes. The boys would always carry a long pointed stick and strike the snake if they saw one moving in the grass. Margaret and her siblings had never forgotten the time, two years before, when a boy of eight years of age had died after he was bitten by a rattler while picking berries on the hill above his house. From that day forward, even the sight of berries brought this ugly memory to Margaret's mind.

The men were paid with script which was money from the coal company. It could only be used to buy a few things from the company store and to pay the rent for their house which was owned by the coal company. It was only in later years that Margaret learned that the store items were overpriced and between rent and a few essentials, there wasn't much left.

There were no stores in the area other than the company store. The miner's families didn't have money to spare and there were very few things to buy at the company store in the hollow. Families just had to make due with what they had on hand. Food was grown in vegetable gardens and canned before winter set in and then stored in the root cellar. The family ate mostly dried beans, cabbage and cornmeal. Mother purchased flour in large sacks. After the sacks were empty, they would be used for clothing. Lard was hog fat and purchased and used for baking biscuits, a main staple. Fruit was available in the summer and what they didn't eat, they canned. Whenever the boys went hunting and brought home rabbits or squirrels that would be the fresh meat for their meals. Some people raised hogs to make their living. The stench from their house was awful, especially in the summer when it was hot. It was so bad that the pig farmers couldn't get the awful smell out of their clothes. Every fall a hog would be slaughtered and the meat hung for hours in an old shed out back being smoked for hams.

Coal was used to heat the houses and for cooking. The floors were bare wood with rugs made by plaiting strips of rags together. These little rugs helped to keep the floors warmer in the cold winter months. Nothing was ever wasted. Soap was made from hog fat and lye and was very harsh on the skin, however it was cheap to make and washed clothes and dishes well. *Ivory Soap* was hoarded and only used for babies and little children's tender skin to bathe with on Saturday night. Margaret's family was as poor as church mice but they were good God fearing people who worked very hard from daylight to dark. They were close knit and supported each other through many hardships. Together they sought out each others strength and overcame the challenges they faced each day.

5
working in the mines

The mines were the only place to make a living in Burnwell, West Virginia. The pay was low and the families were large. The people were dirt poor but they were used to it. Generations upon generations had lived this kind of life and many had managed to survive. The years of the Great Depression were a time with many people learning to make do with much less. Families slept together on one over-crowded bed, some even at the foot because there was no room at the head. Often a pallet made up on the floor with blankets and home made rag quilts substituted for a bed. Meals made out of lard, flour and beans with sometimes, if they were lucky, meat from wild animals. Any wild animal such as rabbits, squirrels or wild boars were eaten. Soup lines were common in cities to feed the hungry. There were few jobs available and many men were unemployed. The miners were considered lucky to have a job at all. Most people went to church and tried to hold on to their faith in God. The children were the ones to always find joy in this day-to-day harsh living.

They smiled happily and went about their business of playing with the other children with no worries about the future. As the years pass, they began to understand that life could be harsh sometimes and they would begin to lose the playfulness of childhood. Margaret remembered the fear on the faces of the miners as they went to work to feed their families. Families kissed and hugged one another, before they went to bed each night, never knowing if their love ones would ever come back home from the mines the next evening. Perhaps death would separate them forever.

At the mining shaft were railroad cars all around the area. The mined coal was put directly into the railroad cars and shipped all over the country. The mine was dark and dreary and the opening looked like a cave with a platform in the center. The platform had a railing around it and was actually the elevator that brought the miners below ground at the beginning of the shift and to the surface when the shift ended. Coal miners would get up before the light of day to descend into the bowels of the earth to remove the filthy black bituminous payload. Coal was the lifeblood to so many who counted on it to provide for their families. It was a dangerous job with explosions and cave-ins with very little personal protection devices, all of which made the job treacherous.

It had been three years since the last tragic accident happened deep down in the dark cold earth. Twenty men had died as a collapse in one of the mine shafts occurred. It took a whole week before the bodies could be brought back up to be buried in the old cemetery next to the Baptist church. The entire community waited and prayed with the families. It was the longest week Margaret had ever known and she hoped that somehow the men would be found alive. Everyone else was thankful that it wasn't their own husband, daddy or son. Yet, in spite of the fear, men still had to return to work in the mines. When the emergency whistle would blow everything in town would stop whatever they were doing. In a panic the people would rush to the mine site in hopes of hearing that their loved ones had been spared.

It was once said that a U.S. soldier fighting in World War I had a better chance of surviving in battle than the coal miners did in West Virginia while working in the coal mines. If you did manage to survive the hazards of working in these dangerous conditions, your life expectancy was under fifty years of age as the constant breathing of the coal dust would take its toll on a miner's lungs. Sometimes men worked 200 feet below the ground down in the mines in total darkness. Coal dust covered everything and it also filled the air affecting all the people who lived there, not just the miners. A condition called "Black Lung" disease helped to shorten a miner's lifespan. This disease caused younger men to age well before their time. Unable to breath they would finally collapse to their deathbeds. This would happen just about the time the first grandchild was starting their first days on the job. Young men followed in the footsteps of their father and grandfather. Whole families worked together with uncles and even grandfathers to support a single household. It was a vicious cycle, with no end in sight. The miners were unsung heroes whose work made life more bearable for many others but not their own

6
socializing

When you live in a coal mining town, such as Coal
Burg, West Virginia there are only a few places to social-
ize and one is the company store with the church and
school being the others. Margaret had been so proud the
day she started first grade at school. She really enjoyed
learning her ABC's and loved the stories the teacher read
to them. The school building was small and contained
only two classrooms. It was rundown and shabby with
no paint on the wooden boards framing the outside the
small building. All the children attended here from first
through the eighth grades. School could, at times, be a
fun place for most children. They would enjoy being with
the other kids and learning to play many different games
at recess like *Red Rover* and *Jacks*. Some of the girls liked
to jump rope while the boys enjoyed playing ball games.
Most children had many chores to do at home, however,
during their brief time at school they could just be children. This could be a good time for children to be taught
of far-off places. How sad Margaret was when she had to

finish the eighth grade. She knew that her education was all over and though disappointed she understood she was needed at home to help her family.

The war was raging in Europe and most of the boys, at age sixteen lied about their age, joined the military. There was a small Baptist church about a mile down the road where young people enjoyed going as there was not much else to do. Most families tried to do their housework and other chores on Saturday so that they could attend church together on Sunday. Sometimes the boys would ask to walk some of the girls home after the church service. There was one boy that had been Margaret's friend from the first grade on up. His name was Howard Jones and they were in the same room together at school.

Like Margaret, Howard also came from a large family. Howard was not especially good-looking but his kindness and warm attitude made him especially attractive and fun to be with. Margaret and Howard would often dream of a life outside of Burnwell and shared their aspirations for a better life together. Coal mining was not a high paying job and Howard knew that, like many generations before him, he too would have to drop out of school now and to help with the support his parents and younger siblings. Together the two of them often shared deep feelings for their families and each other as they walked along.

Each year they seemed to grow closer together as good friends. Sometimes in the summer, they would go swimming in the creek adjacent to the school which flowed down from the high mountains that surrounded the town. The cool, winding creek offered the only relief from the burning heat in the long days of summer. Under the watchful eye of older siblings, younger children at times would sit upon the embankment and dangle their feet in the water and splash one another. Others collected rocks and tadpoles at the creek's edge, screaming out in excitement at their findings. The school kids would at time share a picnic lunch and get to know one another better. Howard was always wanting to be near Margaret. He was the only boy she had ever looked at and she thought she was to be the only girl for him. The attraction between them was plain for all to see. Young love can be so strong at times, yet it is sad that the future can not always be predicted. Life does not always be as one had hoped for.

7
dancing with howard

Margaret's biggest joy in life was her family and thinking about Howard. Her father had a stern way of speaking and his word was the law. All of the Weaver children obeyed their parents as they didn't want to be punished by his big hand or to get a "whooping" out back in the woodshed. In spite of his way of raising us children, we all knew that we were the apple of his eye. Margaret's father had developed a constant cough at a young age due to breathing the coal dust. It seemed to also be embedded deeply in his skin. Even after washing up with lye soap, he never seemed to look clean. He was bent over from the waist and could not stand straight up most of the time. Sometimes Margaret would take his shoes off for him after he came home from work and rub his feet. She felt so sorry for him because in spite of his toughness he appeared to be worn out.

Margaret and her mother would work most days from dawn to dusk in the kitchen trying to feed all of the many children. Biscuits had to be baked everyday and so a fire was started in the stove with coal brought from the outside shed before daylight. Breakfast was prepared early so Dad could eat before going off to work in the early dawn. "Up before the chickens," he would say laughingly. Gravy with biscuits and mush would sometimes be their breakfast. There would not be any lunch. For supper they mostly had pinto beans and cornbread. Mom also worked in the garden all summer and fed the family corn and tomatoes and canned the rest for winter. Margaret did a lot of the housework and scrubbed clothes on a scrub board until her fingers at times were raw. She carried a baby on her hip most of the time as one was always crying for her to hold them.

Square dances were held at the schoolhouse about once a month. People were hungry for fun and relief from the hard back breaking work. Sometimes both young and old would gather together for a foot stomping time. They kept time to the music using pans and lids and buckets were turned upside down and used as drums. An old fiddle and banjo made sweet music to a dreary existence as no one had a record player or a radio. Margaret and her friends clapped their hands and stomped their feet and for a while all was well with the world. From one month to the next Margaret counted the days and tried to find pretty clothes to wear to the square dance. Square dances were the very best times of her life and the country music made her feel young and alive.

There was joy when the room was filled with the sound of country music. The girl dancers twirled around dressed in full skirts. Even little girls who could barely walk tried to tap their little feet to the music. Some people danced their favorites like the Virginia Reel. There was always a person "calling" the dances in a sing-song voice. They would call out the next steps and the dancers would twirl their partner around the square. Everyone clapped their hands and stomped their feet. Margaret danced with different boys but it was Howard that she enjoyed dancing with the most. It was he that she kept thinking about as they were friends connected from their first day at school. They were dance partners and Margaret often hoped that someday they would be even more, like husband and wife. Her deep feelings and love for Howard was now more than just a childhood fantasy. His very touch aroused fire and passion at the core of her soul. When Margaret danced she felt like a beautiful girl, a princess, twirling and floating around with her eyes closed and her skirt would flair out all around her.

White-haired women and grey-haired men tried at these dances to forget the drudgery of the coal mining life. Some boys stood on the side lines as others picked the girls that they wanted to dance with, the one that each hoped to escort home later that night. Life was simple and good as most basic needs were met and the need for survival was forgotten. At times there would be young people coming here to Burnwell to the dances from other nearby small towns. A few of them drove old cars but very few people however had enough money for a luxury like a car. Many people would sit on each other's laps and squeeze into the small seats because the cars were crowded. Getting a car ride was a special treat for everyone involved as many folks never got such an opportunity.

8
turning sixteen

One day Margaret realized that she was growing up into a young woman as her clothes were beginning to be too tight. At times she would gaze into the mirror and say to herself *I wonder if Howard thinks that I would make a good wife?* Her hair was long reaching to her shoulders and she would pull it back off of her face most of the time with a ribbon that matched her dress. When she could get a yard of ribbon it was her luxury. The only gifts she ever requested were pretty yards of ribbon. Margaret was the only one in the family to have dark brown hair and blue eyes. At five feet two inches, she was a full inch taller than her mother. Everyone else in the family had dark blond hair and brown eyes. She guessed that she got blue eyes from her Grandmother Weaver on her dad's side of the family. Dad always told her that she was so pretty and looked just like his mother.

Margaret hoped that she looked pretty and she wanted to look good when she went to church. She hoped Howard would like how she looked. She would stay up late after everyone else went to sleep on a lot of Saturday nights sewing for herself. She decided that she needed some new clothes because she didn't want to wear her mother's hand-me-downs anymore. Life was difficult, but it was all Margaret had known. In a coal mining town everyone was poor. Their main task was to put food on the table. People grew tired and children grew up and continued on with the same life that their parents had lived. There seemed to be little hope of a better life unless one moved away and left family and friends. Which most people did not want to do and only the brave attempted.

That summer Margaret turned sixteen and she had never been so happy for her birthday to arrive! Her mother bought her a matching pink bra and panties. Her mother had saved for months to surprise her with this very special gift. Of course no one could see them, but Margaret knew they were there and they made her feel extra special as she dressed to go to church on the next Sunday. Most of the girls would gather on one side of the church building while the boys gathered on the other. Margaret felt her face burn whenever she caught Howard looking at her from across the aisle. She would sometimes smile at him and look quickly away. This however was not the first time she had felt this way with Howard. She knew her heart beats fast at every glance.

"What is wrong with me? I've known him most of my life. We've been friends since the first grade. He seems to get cuter every time I look at him. Maybe it's the way his hair is parted on the side. No, it's the color of his brown eyes with the dark lashes. I must quit thinking about Howard and listen to the preacher. After all, I'm in church! God's house Maybe he will ask to walk me home from church today. Maybe even hold my hand. I think I'm going crazy!"

The church was one mile down the road from Margaret's home. After church the congregation would walk-the whole way home. The women would walk with the children and the men would walk together and discuss politics and the war. Their loud voices could be heard above the children's. The war was on everyone's mind these days. The older girls would pair-up with each other and sometimes the boys of their age would step up with the girls and then as a couple would walk home together. When Margaret came out of the church the sun was brightly shining and the day was beautiful. It was early July and the weather was warm and pleasant. A few boys were waiting outside of the church building but Howard came directly up to Margaret and said, "Margaret, mind if I walk you home?"

Margaret was so amazed that she almost dropped her purse but somehow managed to smile and say, "Yes, I would like that, Howard." She had been his friend for so many years, however, for some unknown reason she became tongue-tied Unable to say one word, *dreams do come true*, she thought as the two walked along in silence for a while. Howard said, "I just signed up for the Army." A burst of tears flowed down her cheeks as her hands tightly clutched his. Such pain can leave a person at a loss for words.

Margaret didn't say a word, so he continued "I'll be leaving in two months to go to boot camp."

She just stared at him. *Oh no,* she thought to herself. *What will I do if I can't see him?*

Howard said, "I'm a man now. I need to fight this war and help protect my country. I do want you to know that I will miss seeing you most of all. You are a part of me, you know? We have been close all of our lives. Do you think your dad would let me call on you? You're the only girl for me, Margaret. I think you know that."

Margaret couldn't believe her ears. *He wants to call on me!* First her heart began to break at just the thought of him going away. Then her heart was bursting with happiness when he asked if he could call on her. Her prayers had surely been answered.

Every night for the past two years Margaret had prayed and asked God for this sweet man. Now he said she was his only girl. *Can life be any better than this?* She smiled and told him that she would ask her parents if it was okay if he could come over to their house tonight. The walk was over much too fast and Howard said goodbye at her door and went home.

As soon as Margaret's family sat down to eat dinner after church, she asked her parents if Howard could call on her later that night. They said yes and then she immediately sent her brother Gene to give him a note at his house. Margaret sang a song of joy as she washed up the dinner dishes. Her mother and father rested in the afternoon when all the little ones took their afternoon nap. Her sister, Maxine knew of her deep feelings for Howard as together they had shared everything ,including their bed. Maxine helped her clean up the kitchen and to straighten the parlor furniture. Maxine also helped her fix the dress she was altering on the peddle Singer sewing machine. All of their clothes were either hand made or hand-me-downs as money was just too scarce. The dress Margaret was working on was made from a flour sack. Maxine was pressing the hem on Margaret's new dress as she was trying to put a new blue ribbon in her hair. Her smaller siblings were playing a game and being very good for their sissy. Everyone could feel how happy she was and it seemed the whole household was full of joy. Mom even baked a lemonade cake as a special treat.

Tonight would be the first time that Howard would be invited to see Margaret as a beau. When the time finally arrived, she answered the door. He looked so sweet standing at the door with a bouquet of yellow buttercup flowers for her. After he said hello to her and all her family, everyone disappeared and suddenly they were alone in the parlor. They sat down and had nothing to say for the longest time. Then they laughed because they both started saying something at the same time. The ice was broken! Why were they acting this way? They had been such good friends for years but now things were different.

9
a pledge of love

Howard began talking about going off to war and leaving behind his family and friends. People who lived like Margaret and Howard's family rarely went anywhere and here he was talking about going across the sea to another country. Then he would fight in the war and possibly be killed or injured. He seemed sad and excited all at the same time. Life as they knew it now was about to change and this made them fearful. He took her hand in to his and said that he would write her letters every day. She was all choked up and could feel the tears spill down over her cheeks. He squeezed her hand tighter and whispered, "Don't cry Margaret, I didn't mean to make you sad. I'll miss you most of all, my sweet love. I must now tell you how I feel. You are my sweet love, my girl. You have always been the only girl for me. Do you think you can wait for me? Could you be mine? After I come home from the war, if you would have me, perhaps we could get married."

Margaret's heart stopped! She took his hand in hers

and said, "You have made me the happiest girl in the world, Howard. Of course I'll wait for you. There is no other love for me."

The hours passed so swiftly and it was time to say goodnight to Howard and she walked him to the door. For just one moment, it felt as if they were the only two people in the world. They stood looking at each other and then he moved his head slowly toward hers, bent down and their lips touched ever so gently. Margaret's stomach did flips flops. This was their moment...their very first kiss. She never wanted to let go and as they separated slowly, Howard said to her, "I love you Margaret."

Margaret watched him walk down the porch steps all the way until he disappeared from sight. She then turned and went back into the house. It took a minute for her to realize what had just happened...then, she flew up the stairs to the room she shared with her sisters. She had to tell them all about the wonderful news she had just heard from Howard. Perhaps they would be married after he came back home. She could not seem to close her eyes because her mind whirled with excitement. She laid awake for hours going over the whole evening and everything they had talked about. She must have just fallen asleep when she heard her mother call her name. "Margaret, it's time to get up and help with breakfast, a new day begins."

Margaret ran down the stairs—her feet barely touching the floor. "Mother, I'm so happy. Were you this happy when you first met Dad?" He said maybe we could be married after he comes home from the war. Mother smiled and said "Yes dear, I know how you feel and I'm happy for you, but for today there is work to be done.'.

Margaret concluded that she had to be the luckiest girl in the whole world and started to sing as she dressed the little children and helped them with their breakfast.

So beautiful to her were all their sweet little faces as they watched her dance and sing that morning. Life can be so good when you are young and happy and in love. It's the silver lining in a cold grey world of war. On this day in early June, to Margaret the flowers were glowing in bright red and gold along the fence in their back yard and the birds sang their morning song so sweetly. It seemed to this young girl that her happiness was almost contagious as the little children smiled. Her mother sang more songs as she did the chores through out the day.

Howard and Margaret only got to see each other at church and every Saturday night when he would come calling on her. Then, much too quickly it was time for him to leave for boot camp in North Carolina 500 miles away. He would go with ten other boys from their area and from camp they would go off to the war somewhere far away, perhaps even to Germany. It was almost assured that some of the local boys would be injured or worse... wouldn't come back home at all. That thought was too sad to think about.

When the fateful morning finally arrived many of the families gathered together at the train station to say goodbye to their sons. Margaret felt that her heart would burst with sadness as she kissed Howard goodbye, hoping it would not be their last kiss. She waved and watched the train begin to move away from the station. Her eyes were full of tears as the train pulled out of sight and she could no longer see it or hear it. She stood near the tracks feeling so lost and alone. The crowd grew quiet and no one talked. Each family slowly dispersed and returned to their respective homes, each with their own unspoken thoughts and fears for the future.

Margaret wanted to be alone but in her house that was nearly impossible. There were too many people packed together in one small place and so she busied herself with the little ones at home as usual. There was always a need to care for with this many children. *I guess you can't die from a broken heart,* she thought. It hurt just so much to see him leave on that train, not knowing when she might ever see him again. She already missed Howard and felt that nobody could understand how bad she ached inside. Margaret had promised to write him everyday, so that first letter was written as soon as she had tucked all the little ones into their beds later that night. It begin with the words *"Howard, how many ways can I tell you that I love you? My heart is breaking because I miss you so much. I hated to see you get on that train. I can't bear the thought of you being in danger."*

In her day dreams she would close her eyes and pretend that she would be speaking to Howard. *"My love, when you come home from the war could we perhaps move away to a city, about ninety miles from here, to Charleston. We could have a nice wedding with lots of beautiful flowers in our little church. Red roses could be picked from Mama's back fence, if our wedding is in spring or summer. All of our family members , all of our neighbors and friends will wish us well. Some day maybe we will have a little house with painted boards on the outside. We' maybe could have water in the kitchen, and a bathroom with a toilet, instead of an old out house, such as we, have had all of our lives."* She had such wonderful dreams of having children and a story-book life with her and her sweetheart Howard.

After about two months she had received only two letters from him and they both arrived at the same time. She ran and hid upstairs away from everyone as she wanted to devour each and every word and read the sweet lines over and over. She almost wore the paper out as she crumpled them together in her hands. Her life was kept busy at home, caring for the family each and every day. Her thoughts however were across the water somewhere in Europe where Howard was stationed. She prayed for his safety every night and asked God to please protect him and bring him home safely to her.

She tried to keep extra busy while working with her mother as she wanted to pass the days and hours quickly until she could finally be alone to reread her letters from Howard and write to him daily. She told him how much she missed him and also described all the pretty colors of flowers growing on the side of the hill where they used to walk. She wrote about the little chicks that had hatched in a pen that her brothers and sisters had fixed in the back yard next to the garden. She hope he would to enjoy hearing about all these silly things back home. He didn't tell her much about all the things that happened overseas in Europe. But he did say that sometimes he would go to different towns and meet some of the locals with guys from his troop. He was learning to speak a few words in foreign languages including German.

10
a secret revealed

Margaret couldn't believe it but the months passed and she seemed to grow older. Finally, after two long years and many letters written and received, he would be coming home at last.

Her joy knew no bounds when she read the words "Coming home"! *He's coming back to me.* She thought that she could never be more blessed. She couldn't, however, understand the sudden change in some of his letters in the last few months. She missed him so much and could not wait for them to finally be together. She had poured out her heart to him and wrote letters every day. Then, for two weeks she received no letter from Howard. She kept up her side with writing but no answer came from him. She wondered what could be wrong and she was frantic. Maybe the letters had been lost in the mail some how. Maybe he was just too busy to write at this time. She went from the joy of being in love to fear like a mad woman.

Finally the day arrived that Howard would be coming

home. She stood on the landing at the station not believing her eyes, his train was pulling into the station. Margaret watched with joy as some of the young men began to get off of the train. She stood watching, for Howard's sweet face to appear. Some of the men had brought back wives with them. Many had met girls in Europe and were bringing them home to meet their families and to start their own families.

Suddenly, Margaret looked up and found Howard's sweet face looking at her. Her heart stopped as she ran to meet him. It was then she noticed that his arm was around the waist of a blonde girl at his side. The girl clung to him as they stepped off the train together. He met her gaze and took a step closer. he said, "Margaret, I'd like you to meet Hilda, my wife." At a loss for words she stood in stunned silence. No words could come out of her mouth. Finally, she heard him say, "I did write a letter to you. Then I tore it up. I didn't know how to tell you about her...us. It just happened. I didn't mean to hurt you. Please find it in your heart to understand, war makes us different. The world over there causes people to change...to want different things. "

Margaret turned away, leaving him and his new wife standing there. Nothing could ever mend the ache in her heart that day. She ran all the way home and she crawled under her bed and cried until there could be no more tears to cry. She felt she could never smile or be happy ever again in this life time. Her family tried to comfort her but what can be said to mend a broken heart. Nothing but sorrow and suffering that seems to go on forever. Even the little children grew quiet and didn't laugh or play when she was taking care of them. It seemed like a dark cloud hung all over the whole world and her life was forever to be doomed.

She could never see herself caring for a man ever again.

There could be no other man for her. She would just be a slave for her family and never go out with friends or enjoy people her own age. She refused to go to church or open the door to anyone who came to her home to see her. She just hid away in her misery and told herself that she would grow old with a broken heart. What a cruel fate!

11
starting over

This deep, dark depression seemed to last for about two long years. After making several attempts to get Margaret to attend the square dances at the school her friends and family finally gave up asking. She had lost so much weight that she had to make a few new dresses to wear as her clothes were falling off her skinny body. She tried on the new dresses and looked in the mirror and wondered who the stranger was looking back at her. She pushed the hair from her eyes and stared at herself and wondered who she had become and where her life was going. She had wasted too many months being depressed and she was getting nowhere. New thoughts began to take root and helped her make some sense about her life.

Grief was not going to change anything but it would make her grow older. One day Margaret finally came out of her bout of despair and it was like a sudden awakening from a deep sleep. Her hands shook so much that she could hardly get dressed when she realized that somehow, she had to get back to living once again. She knew a lot of people, including school friends that she hadn't seen in the past two years of her mourning would be very surprised to see her. Margaret thought, *a person has to start anew, somewhere.* She was determined to go and make the best of things but she hoped that Howard and his wife would not be at the dance tonight. She then decided to wash her hair and find some shoes, put on the new dress and go to the dance and be with people her own age. It was time to begin her life again.

Her family was astonished to see her dressed to go with them that night. Relieved to see her coming back to life they hoped she would be more than just a shadow of the fun-loving girl she used to be before her great fall. They didn't know what to say to her. Some laughed, and some were quiet and afraid that they might say the wrong thing that could discourage her from going with them to the dance. Some felt fearful, for what would happen if she ran into Howard and his new wife?

Oh well..., Margaret felt that she couldn't hide away any longer. It must be faced as they lived in a very small town. Today would be the first day of the rest of her life. She had read this saying somewhere and hoped that it was true. *Let the day begin!* Her steps were slow as she heard the music being played inside the school house.

All eyes were fixed upon here as she walked into the room. People grew quiet for a few seconds as Margaret scanned the room for Howard and his wife but was unable to find them in the crowd. And for *this* she was grateful. She could put that meeting off a little while longer.

Margaret could hear the music and her mouth went dry. Stepping into the room she looked around quickly to see who she knew there. To her surprise there was a strange woman with blonde hair, when she saw Margaret she ducked her head. That's when she knew who she was looking at but she couldn't believe her eyes. For a few minutes her world stood still and her heart began to pound. It felt as though it would come out of her chest. It was Howard's wife, Hilda. Howard was coming up to Hilda with a glass of lemonade, his back was to Margaret. Noticing the look of fear on his wife's face, he turned to see Margaret and her family enter the room. Howard turned white and took away the glass of lemonade from his wife. Quickly he went to retrieve her coat and the two of them fled the dance. How Margaret's heart ached to watch, as the two of them left the room together. The whole crowd of people were deadly silent for a few moments, then the music began to play once more. The crisis was over for tonight. Life *can* go on despite heartache and disappointment

Living in such a small town as Burnwell, it would be almost impossible *not* to run into them every once in awhile. She knew she must get used to the pain of seeing them together. She knew it would be very painful but she also knew she needed to live again or else she would die. The choice was now clear to her. Her mother saw the exchange of looks between the couple and her daughter. She knew the way it had rocked Margaret's world and so she turned to her daughter and said, "You are a strong girl and you must get over your hurt. Dance and enjoy your life, you are still young. Heartache does not kill a person." Margaret wiped away the tears from her cheeks and smiled back at her mother. She said, "I am going to try, today is the beginning of a new life for me." The fiddle player struck up a new song and people clapped their hands and some people began to dance once more. She really did feel better now that the ice was broken. She was out among the living at last!

A boy named Jim, whom she had known all her life came over to her. He grabbed her hand pulling her onto the dance floor to join in the Virginia reel, one of her favorite dances. Once her feet began to move, her skirt twirled and she knew somehow she would survive.

The night passed swiftly and as she crawled into bed, she promised herself that she would live her life for her family and that no man would ever break her heart again. It was fun at the dances but there would be no more than friends with the men whom she danced. *"I will probably be an old maid"* she thought. *That couldn't be so bad, now could it? It is better than heartache!*

12
disgracing the family

Margaret passed the time by helping her mother raise the little children, keeping food on the table, and making and mending clothes. About once a month Margaret went to a square dance. Some nights most of the family would stay home and so she would go alone. She noticed a few other young men from another nearby town had showed up. One was in his own car. He was tall and handsome with light brown hair and grey eyes. He kept watching her and asked one of her friends what her name was. Finally, he asked her to dance. He twirled her around and she noticed he had a very nice smile and he also dressed better than most of the guys in her town. When the night was almost over, he asked her if she would be at the next dance. She told him that she tried to come to most of the dances. Then he asked her if he could see her home. She immediately put a stop to that! *No way*, she thought, *she wasn't interested in a beau!*

Time passed and at the next dance he showed up alone in a nice car and he was looking good! He had a very nice smile and she learned his name was Wyatt Kendall from the next town and that his family was well to do. His father owned part of the railroad and he had a very good job with the railroad. She finally agreed to let him drive here home that night in his new car. This began to become a habit.

He kept coming to see her at her house and was very polite to her brothers and sisters. Finally, he convinced her to see him and be his friend. She had told him about her heartbreak with Howard and he understood her fear but he would never hurt her. So the rides started, then picnics under the trees. One day he brought some wine and they sipped it and became relaxed. He began gazing into Margaret's eyes with desire and passion. Her heart began beating uncontrollably and without thinking, she did nothing to stop him, when he grabbed the zipper and tore her dress. The sound of the cloth rending beneath his fingers caused Margaret to gasp in both shock and excitement. Her excitement caused fire to spread to his gut.

"The first time I saw you... His breath was already short and fast when he tossed her mangled dress aside and cleared the remaining piece from beneath her leg.

"From the first minute I saw you, I wanted this. I wanted you." She gasped, "I know." And reached for him, amazed at how deep and ripe a need could be. "Me, too---it's insane." Her skin trembled as he tugged her bra straps from her shoulders and gently removed her cotton panties. He began to tenderly kiss her lips and caressing her breasts with his large rugged hands. Glorying in it, she arched against him and hungered for more. He couldn't stop himself from taking and she could not stop herself from giving. Locking her legs around him she took him in.

Moments later both fear and despair overcame her. How could she have been so foolish to let her guard down? Sin can be so enticing. So bad yet so good.

They had lost all track of time. What had she done-
-Oh no! She had slipped. There was no turning back and
no one must ever know! He promised her he would never
tell anyone and that it would not happen again. As he left
her at the door, she hoped no one would see her as she
crept up the stairs to bed. She felt like such a sinner and
unclean. "Please, God, it is like a bad nightmare. Please
make it all go away", she prayed. She vowed to never see
him or any man again.

She stayed home pretending to have a headache on
the night of the next two dances. Some people began to
wonder where she was. Her friends told her that Wyatt
had been at every dance looking for her but he didn't
come to her house. She guessed that he felt bad about
what had happened between them.

About a month later she really did start to get head-
aches and then an upset stomach. She didn't connect the
problem until she smelled some bacon frying one morning at breakfast time. She ran outside to vomit and her
mother followed her. As mother wiped her face, Margaret saw a worried look cross her mother's brow. "Are
you okay? She asked. What's wrong with you?" Then
she straightened up and grabbed her arm. "Oh no, you
didn't, did you? How could this be? What a disappointment you are! Who was it? When? Where"?

Mother sank slowly to the ground with her face in her
hands and wept tears of heartbreak. Margaret then realized what her mother meant and it sank in. That one time
of weakness and sin and she would have to pay for this
the rest of her life. "Oh no, it just can't be …a baby. I'm
not married. With no husband, I'll be an outcast. Why
God?"

So many times when disaster comes into your life
to knock you down, you feel that things could never
be worse than they are at that moment. When Howard

brought home a wife from the war, Margaret's heart was broken. For two years Margaret had dreams of being his bride but she was devastated. Seeing him with his arm around another woman was worse than death for Margaret. She had always thought he had been the one boy who seemed to be her soul mate. The man she would share all of her life and dreams with.

After two years of mourning the loss of Howard, Margaret met someone else with whom she shared a stolen moment of sin. Now she could not believe that she could be pregnant. She thought, "No, not me. How could this have happened? I am a not a bad girl. I have hopes and dreams. My family counts on me, they need me." She was the oldest girl in the family. Pregnant, a baby, the thought was just too much to take in. Margaret agonized; she would be the talk of the town. Everyone would know about the pregnancy. How could she have a baby when she is not married and she doesn't have a husband? Her baby would be talked about too. Then Margaret thought about her poor Mother, what about her and Daddy? Margaret felt so ashamed. How could she ever look them in the face? They will be so hurt and disappointed in me. She thought of all her younger brothers and sisters and how she had let them down too. Margaret crawled under the bed and cried until no more tears would come. When Margaret told Mother; she went to bed for a whole day not even speaking to her.

Margaret's Dad came home from work the next day and he and Margaret's mother spent the whole evening after dinner in their bedroom with the door closed. They then called Margaret into their bedroom and Daddy would not look directly into Margaret's eyes. His eyes were red as if he had been crying. Mother asked Margaret, "Please tell us who you have been with and have you spoken with him about this yet?" Margaret began to sob and everything came pouring out about the one time that Wyatt Kendall and Margaret had fallen into sin. Mother said, "You need to talk with him as soon as possible." She agreed to do that at the very next square dance. Margaret sensed that the whole family seemed to know that all joy and happiness had forever left their home. That's how Margaret felt as each one of her sisters and brothers would come to her and ask why everyone was acting in such a strange way. Asking Margaret why Mom and Daddy were not talking. Why was Margaret sad and crying? How could she explain to a child that her whole world had crashed down upon her? She felt as though she could never come out of this dilemma of being pregnant. Margaret would just have to tell them in the only way that they could understand. She'd say, "Guess what? "We are going to have a new baby in this house and it is going to be mine." The children just smiled and didn't ask her to tell them any more about the baby growing within her or who the daddy was.

The work and chores were done and the children played quietly. An atmosphere of doom and gloom had settled in the home. Margaret slept a lot lately; she somehow hoped that she would awaken and find that this nightmare had all been a bad dream. Not so, the nightmare was real and she felt sick with nausea everyday. She was also sick with heartache and shame over the way her life had become such a shambles. Her hopes and dreams lay in the dust. She was so young, yet she felt so old. Perhaps Wyatt would ask her to be his wife. Maybe a quick wedding could take place and they could become a family. Deep in her heart she had fears that this was not to be.

13
grandma's demise

As the months began to pass, Margaret never went out to the store or even to church. A few friends came to the house asking to see Margaret but she would hide away. Someone else would answer the door and send them away, saying that she was indisposed and not receiving guests. Poor Margaret was in a state of deep depression. She was so depressed that she didn't even speak unless she had to answer a question. She worked extra hard around the house, doing chores to keep busy and fill the hours and days.

Finally, that fateful day arrived and as she had promised her mother, this would be the day that she would tell Wyatt her secret. Despite being pregnant, she did not show yet; however, the guilt was overwhelming and she prayed that somehow he would be excited and want both her and their baby. Her feet felt like lead as she neared the school house where the dance was in full swing. The fiddlers were playing their favorite song and she reminisced about the wonderful times that they had when they danced together. How magical it was when he kissed her. She looked around the room a few minutes hoping to find him. Then, she spotted him standing, with a drink in his hand, looking so handsome and sure of himself.

As she approached him, he turned around and their eyes met. His face lit up and he smiled and extended his arm around her waist. Margaret gently removed his hand from her waist and asked to speak with him privately. They walked outside to his car and he asked "what is wrong" and "where she had been at the last two dances". Then she cried and told him that she was pregnant. He wiped the sweat from his face with his handkerchief and paced back and forth. "Margaret, how could this be? It was only one time!" He began to tell her he really liked her and was so sorry but this was a terrible problem. He had a neighbor girl who lived in the house next door, that he was probably going to marry sometime next year. He then left her without another word, got into his car and drove off with her standing there outside the school. The music still playing and her heart fell down to her feet. Life was once more in the mire but this was the worst blow ever to happen to an unmarried girl, She was forever disgraced.

This time her whole life was ruined. Her family would be disgraced and her future forever blackened. What would she do? Nowhere to run, nowhere to hide. Oh what a mess she was in--her home already overflowing with too many people and too many mouths to feed.

About a month later Wyatt and his father came to her house. He looked so businesslike with a hat and overcoat on. They asked if they could talk with Margaret. Wyatt's father took out $800 and handed it to her. He said it was for the care of the baby who was to come. Wyatt would be marrying his girlfriend from his hometown. He wanted Wyatt to forget her and his baby. It was to be born out of wedlock and would be a disgrace to the whole world. With this he drove out of her life forever.

How could anyone who looked so nice on the outside and seemed to be a respectable person come to see her like this with his Father? They both acted so formal offering me money to get their selves off the hook. This was a baby that was going to be born. His own flesh and blood and what about Wyatt's father? This would be his first grandchild. Neither one cared about the baby or her. They wanted to forget that this was a real child. Just a terrible mistake.

She watched them drive away. Wyatt Kendall was married the following Sunday in a little white church in Hansford, a town twenty miles from where she lived. She heard the news from a girl named June Sutherland who lived in the same town that Wyatt was from. June came to visit her uncle who lived near her family. They ran into each other at the company store. June didn't know that she was pregnant but had seen Wyatt dancing with her at one of the square dances. She felt sorry for the girl he married because he was a bad man and a scoundrel. He looked good on the outside but on the inside he was like a rotten egg. Maybe he had no heart. It must have run in the family.

Please God, let my baby have a good heart.

After the terrible shock of finding out that slipping into sin, just one time, would be the ruin of her, she decided to visit Grandma Bosher. She was a little white-haired lady with blue eyes and hair pulled back into a bun. She was barely five feet tall and ninety years old. She had lived in a small, one room shanty about three miles from us. She was a strong woman and had out lived her husband and all but two of her ten siblings, my mom and Uncle Kenneth. He had moved away when he was twenty years of age and went to find a life for himself away from the mines. The family seldom received any word from him except at Christmas. He didn't come to visit his Mother or any of us. After the army, he went to Ohio and started a small business for himself. He had joined the army when he was young.

Grandma Bosher always seemed to be at peace with life. Her only companion was a white cat with blue eyes. She got a small monthly check to buy her food. She said she had few needs and God always provided for her. She refused to live with our family desiring solitude instead. She managed to live without electricity using an old oil lamp and water from a well. Grandma Bosher had an old bed in the corner of the room. A cook stove and small table with only two chairs, a rocking chair and a small cot filled up the room. She read her Bible every morning and you could hear her singing old hymns all day as she tended to her flowers in spring and summer. During the winter months she would piece small scraps of material together for a quilt. She also liked to grow vegetables in a small patch of ground, beside her house. Her shanty was about a mile from the little Baptist Church. Every Sunday she would go with her Sunday best clothes walking and speaking to anyone she met. She went to worship her God. After church she would go to the grave of all her loved ones and say a prayer. All of her family was buried in that one little graveyard.

Grandma Bosher was a great woman who possessed great inner strength and resilience. She persevered through hardship and overcame challenges presented to her time and time again. She was certainly no stranger to grief; however, her faith in God was unshakable and she relied on Him to see her through the dark times. It was the basic foundation upon which her life was built. Margaret knew that Grandma Bosher would understand her circumstance and help her. After weeks of crying and working through her depression, she went to her mother and daddy and asked permission to see Grandma Bosher. She saw the pain in their eyes.

"Do you think I could go to visit Grandma Bosher?"

At first she thought it surprised them when she asked to go. After they talked between themselves, mother said that it would be alright because I wasn't showing yet. Margaret hurried and fed all the little children and cleaned up the kitchen. She then gathered a few clothes into a bag. She didn't know how long she would be permitted to visit Grandma Bosher. She didn't want to upset Grandma Bosher, but she needed to gather her thoughts.

It was almost noon when Margaret walked up to the door of the old shanty where Grandma Bosher lived. She knocked on the door and listened for her moving around inside the house. When she opened the door, she said, "Come right in dear, I have some soup on the stove. We can share a bite to eat together." The look on her face was serene. How wonderful to have a visit from her sweet Margaret. "Please sit down and let us ask the Lord's blessing."

That is when the dam broke and Margaret sobbed out her story. She held her and let her tell everything on her heart. Then she took down her Bible and read the story of the Prodigal Son. telling about God, our Father, who forgives all sin. She also said "some day all that bad would be turned into good." As Grandma spoke softly to reassure Margaret that she would always be there for her, she unfastened a small gold heart shaped locket from around her neck and placed it around Margaret's neck. It was Grandma's most cherished possession given to her by her beloved husband on their wedding day fifty years ago. The locket had always been comforting to her and she felt now was the time to give it to Margaret. Grandma slowly reached out and embraced Margaret holding her closely-- "My dear child, you will never be alone. Please take this as a symbol of my deep love for you. If you keep it close to your heart you will never be lonely or afraid for I will be there in spirit next to you." She shared that she might be old, but she understood how easy it was to slip into sin. Margaret was allowed to sleep that night on the small cot in her bedroom. During the wee hours of the morning Margaret heard her grandmother praying for her and the unborn child.

Margaret felt a little more strength after spending the night with Grandma Bosher. She felt that she was still needed at home to help her mother and dad. Shortly after breakfast Margaret began her trek home but promised that she would come back again one more time before she began to show her pregnancy. Margaret knew that after she grew big with child, she would have to hide away from all eyes. She needed to cover her pregnancy from the whole world but this was not possible. The very ones who mattered most to her, would see her every day and there was no hiding the truth from them.

Margaret was about two months along when she heard a loud knock on the front door just before daybreak. A man stood there and asked to speak to her Dad telling him to please come quickly, because something was terribly wrong with Grandma Bosher. She had fallen down and the doctor couldn't seem to revive her. They thought she had hit her head on a rock while drawing water from a well. We all ran to get dressed after Mother and Dad went with the man, who was a neighbor friend of the doctor. The whole family gathered by her bedside praying for a miracle to occur. She opened her eyes and looked around, then sighed and was gone too fast.

How could it be that Grandma Bosher had died? Grief overcame us and we held onto each other and cried. Then the pastor walked in and asked us to pray with him. We agreed that Grandma Bosher was in a better place and she would now be with all her children and her husband of fifty years. Margaret guessed that they were crying for their own loss.

The sky was blue and the sun shining on the day Grandma Bosher was laid to rest. The church couldn't hold all the people, so many stood around on the outside. She would be buried next to Grandpa and the world had lost an angel. People, one after another, told of the kindnesses and ways she had touched their lives. As she was leaving the grave site, Margaret caught a glimpse of Howard. He had his head bent to avoid eye contact and next to him stood his wife. She was glad she didn't have to speak to them. She really wasn't showing yet, but she felt everyone could tell by looking at her. As fast as she could, she went home and hid away in her bedroom. She needed to mourn for Grandma Bosher in her own personal way. Life had once more dealt her a devastating blow.

14
rosemary's arrival

The months passed slowly as Margaret tried to cope with the loss of her dear grandma. She tried to have faith in God as Grandma taught her, all of her life--but to no avail. She was to broken down in despair. All though she did try to read the bible that grandma had given to her, when she was a very young girl, Margaret felt that there could never be any hope of a good life, for her or this baby that was to be born out of wedlock. Where was God when I messed up my life-- so many questions, so many regrets? Yet ,there was no way out of this terrible dilemma. A person must accept life as it comes, and all of the consequences. Margaret could hardly believe that she had to go through a real pregnancy. She had watched her mother go through nine long months of pregnancy so many times --but to her disbelief, this time, was to be her.

The family tried in so many ways to show her love but she went through many days like a zombie with no feelings. She didn't talk unless she had to say something and just went through the motions. She tried to work extra hard for mother and father and did the cooking and washing most days. The pain and disaster of her pregnancy seemed to have aged her parents ten years overnight but they carried on living as she grew bigger with child. Then one night Margaret was awakened with labor pains. A mid-wife came to care for her as the doctor was with another woman in labor. Margaret was so frightened and felt so alone but she tried to be strong for the other people in the house. The agony built and built until she couldn't stand the pain and she cried out, "God, take my life, let me die. I don't want to live anymore." Then the screaming began, she couldn't believe that it was she who was screaming. Then, just when Margaret had given up all hope the baby came into the world. Margaret was so exhausted, with sweat covering her body. The mid-wife held her daughter up. She was so small and pink and she heard the cry that said she was in the world. Then she was placed in Margaret's arms and she held her tight. Could this be real? Maybe she could find a meaning for life after all. The little mouth moved up onto her breast and caused love to flow to her. *My own baby*, Margaret thought, *God, I guess I do love her, my sweet child.* She counted her toes and fingers, then the little hand clasped Margaret's finger and she held her close.

Margaret's Mother came in to see her grandchild for the very first time. Bittersweet moments followed, a precious baby, a disgrace, and a ruined life, all in one. Tears ran down her Mother's cheek as she held the baby. "She is beautiful and perfect, let me wash her and dress her in pink for you. What will you name her?" Margaret said, "Mother, you pick her name." Mother smiled and said, "She's as pretty as a rose. Let's call her Rosemary." Margaret repeated the name over to herself as she held her and smiled, "Rosemary my daughter! I'm so sorry it had to be this way. Mother I'm so sorry." Margaret knew that she had hurt this family and most of all her mother and dad. How could she make it right? She would give her life to this child and to all of her family whom she loved so dearly. "I promise I won't disappoint you ever again."

For the first time in her life, Margaret was in bed for ten whole days. Back then it was a requirement after giving birth. Her mother took over the care of Margaret and her new baby. The whole family gathered around the bed and seemed amazed with the baby, each one taking turns holding her. Her dad was hurt deeply and Margaret could see it in his eyes but he tried to not blame Margaret too much. He was a man of few words but she felt that he drank too much to cope with the pain he felt over Margaret's ruined life. A few neighbors came to see Margaret, people tried to be nice, a few gifts were brought but she couldn't bear to be seen out in public. She felt that she was meant to be alone, hiding herself away. Time moved on and the baby grew fat and healthy. Margaret's sisters helped care for the baby allowing Margaret to help in the kitchen and the garden with her Mother. It seemed there was never enough hours in the day but somehow they all survived as life went on. Margaret didn't need much of anything. She never went anywhere outside the house. She just worked every day and fell into bed at night exhausted. The next day was no different from the last as she woke up early and worked until late day after day. She wore the same old clothes, the same old shoes, putting cardboard in the soles to cover the holes. She pulled back her hair severely which made her look like an old school maid. She no longer smiled and her once beautiful complexion now lacked color. Once in awhile the baby would catch Margaret off guard and she would have to laugh, Rosemary had a way of looking at her and touching her. She was in her own little world, almost like she had a beautiful life with love and colors but no pain. Margaret's world was now turned upside down. She felt like she was a thorn in her parent's side. She was blessed with a precious, perfect, little baby and yet it was all wrong! Nothing can be right when a woman is an unwed mother. At times she would lie and look at the beauty of her baby's face and she watched her in wonder, as her baby searched for her breast. The little rosebud mouth and tiny fingers and toes made Margaret know, without a doubt, that there was a God, somewhere, that had created this perfect baby girl. At this point in her life, Margaret did not have much faith in God, but she still found herself one morning, whispering a prayer to God, for her baby. She slipped to the floor by her bed and poured out her heart to God. *Dear God, please watch over this little baby girl. Allow her to grow up healthy and strong. Give her a love for the beauty of nature. Teach her to love the sound of soft gentle rain, green leaves on the trees, and bright colored wildflowers that bloom in the springtime. Let her feel the warm, soft grass and the bright sunshine on her body. Please embrace her with your love and grace. Show her all of the beauty of your creation – the leaves turning to red and gold in the fall and the white gentle snowflakes as they paint the world white in the winter time. Allow her eyes to watch the honeybees that swarm in their hives. Most of all, dear God,* she prayed, *please let Rosemary grow up knowing Your love and not grow up to make all the same mistakes I've made. Last of all, dear God; please help me to be a good mother to this child.* Margaret poured out all of her hope and dreams for her baby, to God. Wiping away her tears, she felt somewhat relieved. She was still a broken woman but she was determined to remain in her parents' home. She thought she could work for them and pay her way by taking over most of Mother's chores, as well as her own. Margaret was so ashamed, she refused to go to church or to any outside activities.

She knew she was the talk of the town, so a recluse was what she chose her lot in life to be.

The only time Margaret smiled anymore was when her baby would catch her off guard and would touch her or coo to her. What a sad, sad person she was. She felt like she didn't deserve any joy or happiness, all because of one passionate night. She felt at times like two people in one body. One person wanting so much to have faith in God while the other feeling like a lost cause. "Ruined life" was the way she saw herself with no hope for a future, only shame and guilt. She lived through each day numb and lifeless, eating only to survive, falling into bed at night and sleeping out of exhaustion. This was her pattern of living for many long years.

15
another tragedy strikes

One day, dad said he was moving the family away, because the coal mine was shutting down. Many miners were going to be laid off and out of work. After all his years at the coal mine he was out of a job. He, however, could do strip-mining in another town. So he moved us about fifty miles away to Chelan, another town near Charleston, West Virginia where we were to rent a small house. Four out of the five boys were off serving in the war. Three of the five girls were married and raising a family of their own. Margaret along with her sister, Madge and brother Kenneth remained behind with their mother. We couldn't afford the company house any longer. We were sad to say goodbye to our old home with so many memories both good and bad. All of us children were born there in that old company house in Burnwell.

Our new rental house had only two small bedrooms and used roll-away beds to sleep on in the living room. They were folded up and put away during the day time. My father had to leave us and live in a shanty. He sent money for our mother and us to live on.

The years had passed and Margaret's daughter, Rosemary, started the first grade at school. Margaret continued to work for her mother and earned some money by papering walls and taking in ironing. She ordered some clothes from Sears & Roebuck catalog for her daughter. She never had any clothes or shoes of her own, only what she could use handed down from her sister or mother.

The train track was outside, next to the house and ran most days and nights. What a sad, lonely sound the whistle made. The family's rented house had no indoor plumbing, but they did have running water from a faucet. They still had an old outhouse for a bathroom. They saved ration stamps to buy sugar which was used to make cookies and candies for the service men in the war. We tried to send boxes over seas every few months. They bathed in a tub about the size of a car tire. When they sat in it, their knees would almost come up to their chins. However, at least they felt fairly clean afterward. They had an old ice box for which the iceman would deliver big chunks of ice. This would keep our food cold for a few days.

Some days as Margaret worked, perhaps ironing large baskets of other people's clothes, she would think back over the years since they had moved away. She would think about Howard and wonder what had really gone wrong between them. *Was he happy?* Then, other days she would think of her little girl and herself and the bleak future it seemed they had standing before them. It really didn't matter because she felt like a dead person walking through life. On the other hand her daughter, Rosemary, was a happy child in spite of her beginning. She would skip around and try to catch butterflies in her hand.

Rosemary looked a lot like her daddy, Wyatt Kendall. She had so many of his features, especially his eyes with the same color of blue. Margaret often wondered what happened to him. She had heard that he married the girl next door. *How could he not want to see his daughter?* Rosemary adored Margaret's sisters and her younger brothers. Her mother was the one Rosemary followed around from the time she could walk. She was the center of her mother's life and she would brush her grandma's hair every night from the time she could hold a brush.

Finally, the war ended and all her brothers came home and were able to find jobs. Some also found wives and life became better for them as they were so relieved to be safely home. One night tragedy struck once more when her brother, William, was found dead on the train tracks. They never knew how it had happened though it was suspected he may have been attacked on his way home. A closed casket was placed in the living room at home until he was buried. His death left the entire family shocked, devastated and in terrible pain.

Our sweet mother lost her heart that day as she placed her son in that grave. Life has such agony at times like this. A mother should never have to out live her child. She went to bed for two weeks and refused to speak or eat most of the time. Margaret became the parent and Mother became the child. Margaret would sit by her mother's bed soothing her with some of her favorite Psalms from the Bible--trying to give her a reason to go on living. Rosemary was the only one who, while lying on her bed, would touch her face and say, "Grandma, it's okay, Billy is with Jesus now." Somehow through this love between them, the light came back into Margaret's mother's face again. Little Rosemary loved her back to life. Strange, yet wonderful powers a child can bring upon us grown-ups.

16
raising rosemary

Rosemary would often pick a bouquet of dandelions or violets and give them to her grandma. At times she would make two plaits in grandma's hair after she had brushed and combed it. There was such a bond between her Margaret's mother and Rosemary. Margaret was on the outskirts of this relationship but she was happy to watch their love as it was so entwined. Even though Rosemary had many people that adored her, Margaret's heart would break over and over because her little girl had never known her father. When she started school, she looked so proud going off and waving goodbye because now she was such a big girl! She was growing up so fast and the years seemed to fly by one after another.

A letter came one day from a girl Margaret grew up with. The girl, Jane Sutherland, tried to keep in touch with her after they had moved away. Since Margaret was so depressed, she seldom answered any letters. Jane informed her that Howard's hair had turned grey over night. His shoulders were bent over and he seldom smiled at anyone. He was still working in the coal mines. His wife went back to Germany after they tragically lost their little boy to Diphtheria. Margaret felt sorry for anyone who lost a child and wondered if he felt bad for her or if he just thought she was a sinner. *Can a leopard change its spots? Why did he have to marry that woman? They could have been so happy but poor choices can make life so miserable.* It's like a pebble tossed into a pond and the rings spread in widening circles, so does misery.

There in her grief and sorrow Margaret had tried to find her own happiness, beginning with attending the dances and eventually falling into sin with Wyatt Kendall. This was the biggest mistake of all and she now wished that she had only waited for a nice man to come into her life. She should have waited for marriage and a home of her own. She hurt so badly for her little girl not having a daddy. One day she began to realize that ten years had passed and she was thirty five years of age. Where had all the years gone? She really was getting old! Believe it or not, she was still sleeping with her mother and little girl. People had to share beds in those days.

She felt like she had wasted her life and had turned into an ugly old maid with a child. She never had dreamed that her life would have turned out this way. Her childhood was relatively happy and she had been pretty smart in school. All her hopes and dreams had turned into ashes. *Now look at me with my hair so long and straggly. Clothes just hang on my skinny body. Where will it all end? This existence is not worth living. There is no happiness or joy yet my daughter is so sweet and she is all that I have. Something happens to a woman when she reaches a certain age and gives up on life.*

17
a new job

One day Margaret noticed the bus that ran into a town about thirty miles away. She had heard that people could find work in stores and restaurants there. She began to wonder if this could be possible for her. So she went into town by bus and noticed a sign in the window of a hot dog diner. *Help Wanted, No Experience Needed.* She was so nervous that her hands shook as she had been a recluse for so many years. She scarcely knew how to act around people.

She had cut her hair and borrowed a dress from one of her sisters. She wanted to look her best, realizing she desperately needed this job. She wasn't getting any younger and time was passing her by so, it was now or never. She tried to smile and look friendly when she spoke to the owner and it worked because she got the job! The owner was nice and asked when she could start because they really needed help. Her mouth was dry and she could barely answer. Finally, the owner said she could begin working in two days time. She was in shock and almost afraid to try but she desperately needed to change her life.

She decided to rent a sleeping room for her daughter and herself as this was how many people survived. Rooms were rented with a shared bathroom was down the hall. There was no kitchen or living room space. *It couldn't be worse than sleeping with my mother at age thirty five.* For the first time Margaret and her daughter had their own place. Rosemary seemed to fit in well with her new surroundings. She only wished she could say that life continued on happily ever after. She bought a few new dresses and had a perm put in her hair. Then one day she bought a tube of red lipstick. While looking in a mirror, she almost felt young and decided that she didn't appear so bad after all.

Some of the men who ate at the diner began to notice Margaret. She looked better now with a little color in her cheeks and lipstick on her lips. She also smiled more now and had gained a little weight, however, inside she still felt empty and alone. Some things happen, at times, inside a woman, when she is by herself and so lonesome in her thirties. She begins to realize that she is no longer a girl but a middle-aged woman with feelings and needs that she thought were long ago dead. Her youth has passed her by but the woman in her begins to stir.

With a little help from the other waitresses, Margaret soon caught on to the routine. After all, she had been waiting on people all her life in one form or another. Weeks passed and she started to smile a little more and enjoy her new life. She found that she liked working out among people. For a little while she could forget her troubles and pretend that she was just like others and not a disgrace to anyone. Finally, she began to get used to the work in the diner. Many of the people who ate there were regulars. Everyday a good deal of the same ones came in to have lunch and some came back for dinner as well. They soon learned her name and a few were pleasant and would chat with her awhile.

Her favorite person was a customer named Jim Turner. She caught herself looking up and watching the clock, waiting for him to come in to eat. He had reddish-brown hair and kind, brown eyes. He always tried to sit at her work station, so that she would be the one who served him. They exchanged names after a few weeks and he asked her where she came from. She felt butterflies in her tummy when ever she had conversations with him.

One day he asked if she would allow him to give her a ride home after work. *No,* she couldn't as she was not yet prepared to be alone with a man though she really wanted to go with him but was afraid. She acted a bit foolish, kind of like a frightened rabbit. Then he started to talk about the weather and she felt more relaxed allowing herself to calm down. She finished her shift and was happy to see her daughter's familiar face when she picked her up from school. Rosemary sat at the table that evening and practiced her writing by sending a letter to her grandma.

Dear Granny,

I just had to write and tell you that I miss you. Mama and I are staying in a sleeping room and we get to sleep in a big bed. There is a real bathroom down the hall. There is a nice lady who takes care of me when Mama works. Her name is Mrs. Jamison and I like her.

Hope to see you real soon.

Love,

Rosemary

Rosemary carefully folded her letter and asked her mother to mail her letter tomorrow on her way to work.

After Rosemary had gone to bed, Margaret found

herself daydreaming about Jim. He seemed so nice. She couldn't believe such a good looking guy could really be interested in her. She really was so scared but she knew her fear was because of all the terrible mistakes of her past. She also had her sweet daughter to think of. Rosemary seemed so happy at her new school and had even made a few friends.

18
the road to ruin

Margaret was thirty five and Jim said he was thirty nine and had never been married. She thought she could really like him. She wishes she was a *normal* woman. She had so many failed relationships with men — what was wrong with her? She couldn't go to sleep, and tossed and turned. The next day at work, the hours dragged until Jim came in and sat down. He smiled and said to her, "Margaret, I really do like you. I was wondering if I could have a date with you sometime."

Margaret felt her face grow hot and didn't answer him. He kept asking her and asking her. She wanted to say yes but she answered "No, no, I can't. I have a daughter," she said.

He wouldn't listen to any of her excuses and said "Can't we all go together, to see a movie? Doesn't she like cowboy shows and popcorn?" Margaret quickly turned her head and gave Jim a look of surprise. His question had caught her off guard and she struggled with the desire to be with him or the fear of being hurt again. The question was one of innocence and sincerity. How could she argue with such a kind offer? She, then took a deep breath and reluctantly said "yes".

It was a Saturday and she told her daughter about the nice man that was going to be with them for the afternoon, He was taking them to a movie show. Rosemary was a little shy at first but he smiled a lot and helped them to feel more relaxed. The three of them had so much fun and after the picture show they had ice cream cones.

Margaret continued to see Jim on her days off and felt that she had finally met that one special man for her life. Margaret felt like she was sixteen years of age again when she was alone with this handsome man. He took her for a ride with the top down on his car. The air blew her hair and she felt alive for the first time in years. Suddenly he pulled off the road and darkness was closing in and the moon was shining brightly in the sky. Then he kissed her and chills ran down her legs and she was lost in a world of wonder. His arms pulled her close and she crumbled. Even if she died tomorrow, she must have this night of passion. It took over her and before she knew it, they were making mad passionate love.

When it was over, she was so happy. She wished she could always have this kind of love. His arms, his lips… He took her home and wished her goodnight. This became their pattern as every Saturday they would go to the movies, get ice cream with Rosemary and drop her off to Mrs. Jamisons for the night. Then off they would go to have their time together in his room and she thought she was in love all over again! One day she hoped that Jim would perhaps want more than their Saturdays together. She started asking him about his family and past. He always changed the subject and refused to talk about his personal life. *Why?* She wondered many times. The next Saturday he didn't come to the diner to eat. She watched and couldn't believe that he had missed the whole day.

Being concerned she called his phone but strangely, no one answered. Later that evening she called him again and this time he answered on the first ring and quickly blurted out that he did not want a serious relationship. He had decided to move back to Ohio to his old job. She dropped the phone and ran all the way from the diner to her rooming house. The tears once more began to flow. Her heart was broken and this time could never heal. *So many times she let herself have hope and to dream. Never again-- as there was too much hurt and pain. How could she have let herself fall again? Would the pain kill her?* No, she knew it wouldn't kill her but it would make her wish that she could die.

Margaret had her little girl to live for and she knew her little girl needed her but she felt as though she had let her down. Rosemary asked her where Jim was and she started to cry when she was told that he would not be coming to see them ever again. At work she began to show her grief over Jim. People were too kind to question her but everyone noticed the change in her and work was no longer fun. She started to have a little too much wine after work to relax. Then she began to be late for work because she had become drunk the night before and couldn't get up. One day she didn't go to work at all because of the drinking. The next day when she went in to work she was told that she had been replaced. She had been let go. She started going to a beer garden down the street and met a few people who also liked to drink and play music on the jukebox. In a drunken state she thought maybe this was her answer… just let go and not care. She couldn't be a good person so she might as well be what she was-- a worthless one. She was a bad woman who kept falling in love and being rejected. She always let her family down and there didn't seem to be any hope for her.

Mother wrote Margaret and Rosemary letter every week but she had a hard time answering them. All the lies were growing too numerous to keep track of. She encouraged Rosemary to write letters to her grandma but she told her not to talk about her job. She had just been hired at a beer joint and served to some pretty sad looking people. Most of these were also down on their luck.

Then the day came when Rosemary cried and said, "Mommy, what's wrong with you?" Her daughter started to nag her and question her about being late to pick her up from the movies. Before long there were the complaints about the smell of the wine on her breath, especially when she would throw up from the heavy drinking. Rosemary also complained about their clothes being wrinkled and dirty at times. She seemed like the grown-up and Margaret, the child. She had sunk so low and did not care about her appearance — she became a different person. She tried not to look in a mirror, because she was too disgusted to look at the person looking back at her. The heartache was overwhelming at times. She only could get work part time — the rest of the time, was spent drowning her troubles with wine. However, the pain would always return. She now had to get her daughter away from her and this life that they lived day by day.

19
rosemary and mrs. jamison

Work began to pick up at the beer joint and Margaret was asked to work longer hours. Since Margaret was working so much at the beer joint, Mrs. Jamison asked if she could visit Rosemary and stay with her until bedtime. Margaret was relieved at the offer — knowing Rosemary would be happy and safe. Mrs. Jamison was the age of Rosemary's grandmother and was a widow with no other family. Mrs. Jamison loved feeling needed and showered the young girl with an abundant amount of love and affection. Rosemary loved staying with Mrs. Jamison and Mrs. Jamison adored her right back. Rosemary had a gift for story telling which kept Mrs. Jamison entertained for hours on end.

One day, after baking some ginger snaps together, Mrs. Jamison motioned for Rosemary to come and sit down next to her, on the green high back brocaded sofa located in the small crowded living room adjacent to the kitchen.

"My dear, last week you told me that you had written

a letter to your granny — did you mail it yet?"

"Oh yes! My mother mailed it for me" Rosemary responded proudly.

"It's so nice to have such a wonderful granny and to have such a large family to love you" Mrs. Jamison exclaimed with excitement.

"Did you know that my mother has ten brothers and sisters? She is the oldest in her family...and the prettiest, too!" Rosemary responded gleefully.

Mrs. Jamison placed her hand over her mouth to keep from laughing out loud. "Well, Rosemary, this all sounds very interesting and fun – tell me more about you and your family".

"I don't know where to begin, Mrs. Jamison." Rosemary responded.

"How about when you were three or four years old" Mrs. Jamison suggested.

Rosemary smiled and began her story...

"Once upon a time when I was a really little baby, my mother gave me the name of Rosemary. From the time I was born I lived with my mother and her parents. There were all her brothers and sisters and we all shared one house. I grew up following behind one person or another. Everyone was good to me. Different ones taught me to tie my shoes and how to dress myself. My mother was so busy working with grandma that one of the youngest of the family had to put up with me. As soon as I could walk or talk, I wanted to be big like all the other kids in the family. My uncle was only four years older than me. I waited for him to come home from school to play with me. He taught me how to chase butterflies and after dinner we would sometimes catch fireflies in a jar. What fun it was to grow up with such a large family.

We were poor but I didn't know we were that poor. I guess a warm bed to sleep in and a full tummy is all people really need to be happy in life. Especially if you have people around who

care about you. We all went to church on Sunday and I loved
to hear the singing of so many people.

A man would preach about once a month. He went to different churches on horseback and was referred to as an itinerant preacher. When we didn't have a preacher, one of the townsmen would read from the Bible. I liked the stories he read. In the summer it was the walking home that I really enjoyed after church. Some of the little children my age would all hold hands and walk together.

Then came the day when we were told that we would be moving away. I was scared to leave the house where I had been born but mother said we had to move because papa couldn't work in the mines any longer.

We went on a train for the first time, for a half a day to get to where we would be living. Everyone seemed sad but also a little excited too.

I never had a brother or a daddy either. I guess you don't miss what you never had. I just loved my entire mother's family, especially my grandparents. I wasn't used to being with so many children my own age. I enjoyed coloring in a color book since I was about five years old. Mother would walk me to school on the first day that was about a mile away.

I was okay until some kids began asking me why I didn't have a daddy and why we lived with my mother's family. I didn't know the answer but I felt something was wrong. This was one of the first times I had really stopped to question the answer. I ran out the door and all the way back home.

Everyone was startled to see me. My tears had dried on my cheeks and my hair had come loose from my pigtails that mother had fixed for me this morning. I guess I looked in a state of upheaval. "What has happened?" They all asked together.

Then I poured out the story. How could the answer be told to a little girl who was six years old in a way that would not hurt her so much? Mother and grandma took me into the kitchen. Grandma poured me a large glass of milk. She said, "Sit down here, Rosemary, "I need to tell you a story. You are a very lucky little girl to have so many people who love you. God has placed you in the middle of a whole big family--your aunts, uncles and your grandpa and me, your grandma. You are your mother's special little girl and will be forever."

"There once was a man who could have been your daddy but he made a bad choice and lost out on knowing the sweet little girl that you are. So don't worry little one, God, in Heaven, will always be your Father and that is most special. So tomorrow, when asked about your family, just say, "God, in Heaven is my Father."

The teacher had to tell all the other kids to please leave me alone and not hurt my feelings. The second day I was alright and the years passed and I made friends. I learned to read and write and was a happy little girl. I felt deep in my heart that I was special. I grew to have confidence. I enjoyed skipping and singing and sweeping the dirt around the house to make it look better as no one had any grass in their yards.

I would count the railroad cars as they passed -- one by one. They mostly carried coal to the cities. The trains were noisy and our house sat right next to the railroad tracks.

Mother ironed clothes all day on Tuesdays. She did all of our ironing and also ironed other people's clothes to make extra money to buy me a few new clothes. She also wallpapered rooms for people. She was always busy but always sad. She looked so tired and old because she rarely smiled or acted like she liked anything.

My Auntie Maxine tried to talk to her at times but mother refused to fix herself up or look better. Her other sisters talked about her. I heard them over and over but she refused to change. She said it was too late for her.

Then came a day when I was at school and mother was taken away. I heard the family talking after I went to bed. Grandma said she was sick and would be gone for a few days. She would receive shock treatments to help with her depression and she seemed a little better when she returned.

I think mother had become fearful of people. She then began to speak of maybe going away to work. Perhaps a different kind of life would be better.

I was really closer to my grandma than my own mother because grandma would tell me stories and laugh and sing with me at times. My mother is my mother and we are connected for life no matter if she is a sad person. One of the special memories is the time my Uncle Kenny and I went down to the creek to splash in the water. I think I was about four at the time and he was eight. We pretended to go swimming as the creek was only about six inches deep and it was muddy.

In those days a man would come to your house to take pictures when they reached the age of four. My hair was plastered to my head and I looked a mess. Mother was always pretty calm with me, but this time she blew up and smacked my bottom. She put me in a washtub of water and scrubbed my skin real hard. My hair had to be washed and dried and curled with a curling iron that was heated in the flame of the gas stove. I had to sit very still so as not to get burned.

When the picture man came, I looked pretty good. I always smile every time I look at that picture. My uncle was sent to bed without any supper that evening.

Another memory is the time when I was in first grade and I got home from school and began scratching my head. I had very long, thick hair that most of the time was kept in pigtails. This day, however, I woke up late and didn't have time to get my hair braided. I began to scratch and scratch.

"What's wrong with your head?" Mother asked.

"I don't know," I said.

"Well, let me look at you," Mother said. As she started combing through my hair, she said, "Rosemary, you have head lice!"

I cried out, "Oh, no, what's that?"

Mother said, "Its bugs! We'll have to wash your head really

good. And you won't be able to go to school until we get rid of the lice."

Mother washed my hair in kerosene oil which really burned my scalp and smelled awful. Everyone in our family had to use this special shampoo to get rid of the lice. It went through the school that year but I never got head lice again.

One of the saddest days for me was when my uncle was killed on the train track. My grandma cried and everyone was broken hearted. I was so sad and I was afraid when the casket was brought into our living room for a day and a night. People came to our house with food and stayed up all night. I was called a wake to mourn the dead.

I was afraid the undertaker would put me in a casket also and so I could hardly sleep. Then the big black hearse came and took the coffin to a graveyard where my uncle was buried. Grandma said he was in Heaven now but the body was still in the grave. Life is hard to understand.

Now, one of the happiest times of my life was the day after the World War was declared over. Everyone living anywhere around us gathered outside to dance and beat on pots and pans to celebrate that the war was over. Grandma squeezed lemons and made lemonade using real sugar. We even used ice from the icebox to make it cold.

Everyone was happy and mother seemed to be a different person on that day. She clapped her hands saying our soldier boys would be coming home. She had two brothers in the army and I had really missed my uncles too.

Grandpa came to see us. He had been living up in the hills strip mining to make money. He lived in a shanty and only came to see us about once every four months. He rode a train to celebrate the end of the war with us. How happy can a person be?

We slept crowded in small beds. Some people made a pallet on the floor. Food was scarce but beans and cornbread is very good when you share with your family.

When I grow up, I hope to have a very large family just like my grandma. No matter what she sings to God, I want to be just like her."

Mrs. Jamison began to tear up after hearing Rosemary's story. She gently leaned over and kissed Rosemary's forehead. "My dear, you are quite a story teller and your mother is so very lucky to have such a special girl like yourself You really should begin writing your story in a journal. It would be something for you to always keep when you are a grown woman with children of your own. If you look in my dresser drawer behind you, there is something for you."

Rosemary jumped off of the sofa quickly and opened the dresser drawer and lifted out a small package wrapped in white tissue paper. Upon opening it, she found a beautifully embroidered light blue satin journal entitled "Rosemary's Journey" along with a brand new black fountain pen. Inside Mrs. Jamison wrote "We can not hold a torch to lighten another's life without brightening our own — Thank you my dearest Rosemary for brightening mine, Love, your friend always, Mrs. Jamison".

"Oh — how wonderful!" Rosemary shouted. "I will always treasure this as long as I live!"

Mrs. Jamison knew with all of her heart that Rosemary would and Mrs. Jamison ached for her. At times her mother wreaked of the smell of alcohol, dressed shabby and did little to keep herself clean. Every since being rejected by that man Jim, she seemed to slide further into the gutter. Mrs. Jamison felt helpless knowing that Rosemary's mother was having problems and perhaps would be moving. She dreaded the thought of not having Rosemary around. Oh, please dear Jesus, watch over this precious child and keep her safe.

hitting rock bottom

Margaret found just enough money left in her dress pocket for bus fare for her and Rosemary. All of their clothes fit into two paper grocery bags. Packing their meager belongings made her feel better. She knew some how in her heart, Rosemary would be so much happier living with her mother. So she smiled and said, "Guess what, Rosemary, we are taking the bus to see your grandma today!" Rosemary looked so happy and seemed relieved. She didn't ask and I didn't tell her how long we would be there. Margaret felt so ashamed to let her family see their clothes looking so shabby. She had to find a way to protect Rosemary from the streets and a life of hell and sin. Deep inside she knew that her mother would give her a home where safety and security would be provided for her.

The bus ride was about an hour and the country side looked so clean, beautiful and serene. Freshly mowed hay lay neatly stacked along the silos. Assorted red, yellow and purple wild flowers grew on embankments along the side of the road. When they got off the bus and walked up the lane Margaret's mother came to meet them and they all hugged each other closely. Margaret noticed her mother's shocked expression as she looked at them. Her mother's eyes spoke volumes. Without a word of disgust, her mother welcomed them into her home. The smell of food hit them as they had not had any breakfast or lunch. The hours passed swiftly. Rosemary and Margaret's mother talked and laughed together while Margaret slipped away to give them some time alone.

The night closed in and after Rosemary went to sleep Margaret's mother sat beside her and looked deep into her eyes. Tears streamed down her face. Margaret asked, "Will you keep her here with you? I worry, about her so much!"

Her mother quietly said, "Of course Rosemary can stay here and how about you?"

"No Mother," She said, "I'm on a roller coaster to Hell. I can't bring you down as well, but it's too late for me."

"Margaret, why — please stay, too" she cried.

"No, I'll be leaving in the morning. Don't make this harder than it already is Mother." Walking the floor she wrung her hands. Margaret really needed to have a drink. No, one can fully, understand the life of a drunkard but a drunkard. After they all went to bed, she heard her mother, pacing the floor and praying for them throughout the night. When you live a life of sin, you don't want to live around good, clean and sober people. You cringe and want to try and get far away. Margaret was glad her father had been away for a visit with his brother. She didn't have to fear him this time but she felt like crawling under a rock. She was so ashamed of the woman that she had become.

She loved her family and that made it so much harder for her to look into the good clean life that they lived here.

Early the next morning, her Mother put her arms around her and said, "We are here for you, if you need us." Her mother had become this sweet little Christian woman and she was in need of a drink and hated herself. What she needed was to run away from these wonderful people. They made her feel even worse about herself and it wasn't easy to get away as she dreaded her goodbyes. She held Rosemary close and told her that she did not really want to leave her, but it was in her best interest. All three of them cried and hugged. Then she waited for the bus on the side of the road, like a poor lost soul who wished life could be different. It wasn't long until the bus came and they said their goodbyes once more. Her sweet mother had put her hand into Margaret's purse giving her the last few dollars that she had saved. Margaret's fingers closed around the rolled-up wad of bills. Tears blurred her vision and spilled down her cheeks. How could she have fallen so far into the gutter?

It's so easy to mess up your life. First it was the drinking. Then men tried to make her desirable though she had a bad image of herself. After so many drinks and the loss of yet another job, needing rent money and food made her feel that it would not make a difference if she sinned once more and got paid for it. *This* did make a difference because she felt dirty. She scrubbed her skin raw feeling she would never be clean again. This now became a way of life for Margaret, hanging around on street corners or in beer joints. The faces of the many men became a blur to her memory as one looked just like another. Prostitution was now an everyday part of her life.

21
the awakening

Margaret was now a wino because wine was cheap and helped to dull the pain of her conscience. Then one day a man she had picked up got angry with her because she wouldn't do what he wanted. They argued over it and because they both had too much to drink, he hit her, knocking her down.

When she awoke after being knocked out and spitting blood out of her mouth with broken teeth and blackened eyes, she remembered thinking just how lucky she was to still be alive. She remembered her mother saying "Jesus loves you." I guess He does because she didn't die after that beating and she was amazed that she was alive. The pain was so great and her body ached so much. The man who had done this to her was gone. Beer and wine bottles were lying all around the room. This is how life can be when you live in the gutter and allow booze to take over your existence.

She hid away with a nice lady who tried to help street people. At one time, this lady, Mildred had been one of them and tried to give people a chance to clean themselves up. She ran a rescue center for women and she gave Margaret a job cleaning rooms and cooking meals. The rescue center became her home for about a month. How could it be that she didn't take this chance earlier for a better life? There's a saying in the Bible, "Even a dog goes back to his own vomit." Can a leopard change its spots?" It's not easy. She was trying but after her eyes cleared up and she looked better, she left the shelter and started to drinking once again. One night she asked a man at a bar if he wanted a date. He turned out to be an undercover policeman who had seen her before and he knew she was a street girl. Imagine how she felt when he told her that she was under arrest for solicitation and put handcuffs on her and took her off to jail. Now she had hit rock bottom.

The cold steel bars enclosed her into a world of hell. The jail door slammed shut and she fell across a cot and was instantly repulsed at the filth of the mattress. Walking the floor and wringing her hands in despair, she thought about her miserable life with no job or money. Five other women were locked up in the same cell and some of them had looked over at her in disgust. Even bad women don't like other bad women. They too, feel that women who can sell their bodies are the scourge of the earth. After twenty four hours of being in a state of shock she knew that this was another kind of nightmare... this was the grim reality to her. She had now sunk into the gutter!

This must be faced, somehow. She was locked up in a jail cell with deep depression closing in on her again. Pacing the floor and wringing her hands she cried 'Why, oh why, haven't I learned my lesson? Will I ever? She slipping to the cold floor, "God, she prayed, please just let me die. I can't go on in this life of shame anymore." How much lower can I sink she wondered to her self. Early the next morning my friend Mildred, who had helped many people with a drinking problem and people who had been in jail for minor offenses, came to visit her and said that she would help her one more time. Mildred told Margaret that she had found a job and a sleeping room for her. She said that *this was to be was her last chance so change your life or forever suffer the consequences.* The next morning she was taken to the court room. Her legs were wobbling as fear set in, causing her to tremble. When she was taken before the judge she learned that she could be released if she had a place to go because it was her first offense. She promised to clean herself up and get a legitimate job this time. He released her and said he didn't want to see her back in his court again.

When she stepped outside, it was raining but it felt good. This was, to her a cleansing rain and she felt thankful to be out of jail. She never wanted to go there again. Her stomach was upset and she was fearful because all of her previous attempts had failed. *This time would be different*, she thought. *This time I will succeed. I have been such a failure but, no more.*

She did not know where her strength had come from but she knew she had to find a better way to live. Her daughter and mother must never know the true depths to which she had sunk. She promised herself not to fall into this trap again. She was so grateful that her mother had kept Rosemary for her. They loved each other and had bonded a long time ago. Margaret lost all her possessions while she was in jail so Mildred loaned her a few things until she got her first paycheck.

With borrowed clothes on, she brushed her hair down around her face. It seemed to hide part of her face and because of her bad teeth she didn't smile much. She was fooling herself, though. Anyone could see that she had lived a hard life even if they didn't know all the sordid details.

The next morning she awoke at sun-up. She didn't need to be at work until 10:30 a.m. but she just couldn't go back to sleep. She did have a black skirt but couldn't remember if her white blouse was clean so she checked her belongings which were in a cardboard box but no luck. Then she checked the brown, grocery bag next to the bed and sure enough there it was. She took it to the bathroom sink to freshen it up. After all, she did want to look her best. It was hard to get the wrinkles out but she hung it over the chair in her room. She kept a close eye on it and soon it was dry. She placed it on the bed and pressed it with her hands. It wasn't perfect but it was the best she could do. She told herself that she would get an iron with her first paycheck. *There must be a Salvation Army or Goodwill store nearby* she thought. *I'll check with some of the other roomers.*

She began working at Hal's Hamburgers that day. She knew about working as a waitress from an earlier job but each cook had his or her own way of placing orders. The first day was always the hardest and it took time to get used to the routine. She felt that things were going fairly well but her feet began to hurt. *Darn these shoes,* she thought, they were a size too small and had been given to her awhile back. She was getting by with them but as they were her only shoes and she had to wear them at work they were not exactly good for standing on your feet for six hours a day. Margaret knew she needed to buy a more comfortable pair of shoes along with the new iron. Although her feet and her back both hurt, she was happy to be working with a decent place to live. Most of all she was happy to be starting a new life. This time there will be no men who paid for sex or hanging out in bars. Too much was at stake. She had to stay away from the seedy side of life. She owed it to herself to do the very best she could and *this* would be her last chance.

22
the rocky road back

Things were going along very well when one of the
regulars, a man named John became very friendly and
left large tips for Margaret. He asked her to go out with
him after work, however she wasn't ready and he said
that he understood. John had just been released from the
Marines and had a pension. It was difficult to understand
how he could have a pension when he had two arms, two
legs, two eyes and two hands. They never did get into any
lengthy conversations, because she was always on the
run. Nonetheless, he always let Margaret know that he
was interested in her. This was very flattering, especially
since she felt her looks had left her.

The owner of the restaurant, Hal, was nice to her and
seemed almost like a father to her. He would sometimes
suggest that she should take a break when there was a
lull between lunch and dinner. After several weeks of
working there they sometimes had coffee together and
she opened up and disclosed some things about her
past. It all seemed harmless enough but maybe she had

opened a door for him without realizing it. One night, after closing as they were setting up for the next day, Hal tried to kiss her. She was shocked and dismayed but she really needed this job. What could she do? She pushed him away and said "Please don't do this--I like you but not in that way." At first he seemed angry but after a few minutes he apologized and she was relieved to not lose her job. Though it was never really comfortable working there again she stuck it out not wanting to be fired. Hal acted as if nothing had happened that night but she was always a little on edge when they were left alone to close up the restaurant.

Margaret's biggest fear happened one night when she noticed that Hal had been drinking in the kitchen during the night. First she smelled the alcohol on his breath and then she noticed he began to slur his words. After the last customers had left, she grabbed her purse and headed for the back door which was through the kitchen. Before she knew what was happening Hal came up behind her and said, "Where are you going without saying good-night?" "I'm meeting some friends and they're waiting for me."He turned her around and put his arms around her waist. His foul breath disgusted her and as she tried to back away slowly, he pulled her closer to him and fondled her. She stomped on his foot, smacked him and ran out the door. She was crying and in a state of confusion. *'What will happen now? Do I really need this job?*, she thought.

John then came down the street. "What's wrong?" he asked. She ran to him and poured out the whole incident through her sobs.

"I can't work here anymore. I need this job but what will I do?" John put his arm around her to comfort her and blurted out "Let me take care of you. Let's get married. We can be happy together. We'll go to the Justice of the

Peace."

She couldn't believe her ears. *He wanted me and these were the words I longed to hear. I didn't love him but he seemed nice enough and what did I have to lose? Maybe I could have a home even if it was only an apartment.*

The next morning after a fitful night's sleep, Margaret put on a borrowed dress and met him at City Hall. They were married with two strangers as witnesses. John moved her few boxes of clothing into his apartment. She felt happy and she had high hopes for a better life. At first he seemed to care for her. She thought it was because she was ten years older than he... kind of like a mother. He even had her teeth fixed and bought her some new clothes. He liked the fact that she cooked good meals and kept their little apartment clean and ironed his clothes after all, she had a lot of practice. She even helped him with his medicine dosage.

Margaret met the elderly woman who lived next door to him. Her name was Mrs. Wilson and she appeared to be in her seventies. She was round and short in stature with the sweetest smile on her face whenever she saw Margaret. Margaret liked her instantly but John said that she was a busybody and for Margaret not to be friendly with the likes of her. Margaret was shocked by his attitude and this was her first inkling that he could be an unkind man. It was almost a month before Margaret saw her again. By this time, Margaret had already suffered her first beating from John and he had threatened her to stay in the apartment and never to speak on the telephone and most of all she was to ignore any of the neighbors, especially Mrs. Wilson. Margaret would bump into her when she took out a bag of trash and she always smiled at her but Margaret would turn away and run back into the apartment.

One day, after John had gone out, Margaret heard a

soft rap on the door. She slowly inched the door open and to her amazement it was Mrs. Wilson who stood there. Margaret was so shocked when Mrs. Wilson said, "I am a friend, I live next door and if I can ever help you in any way please let me." Margaret didn't know what to say to her but mumbled that she would and closed the door quickly. Margaret was pacing the floor and wondering what she could do and how to do it. Because a crazy man had beaten her and she'd had her life threatened by him so many times, she collapsed into weakness and despair. After so much abuse by John she was convinced that she didn't deserve to be treated any better and that maybe she should just lie down and take it. However, now there was a ray of hope for her. A nice woman was offering her help! She sat down and wrote a letter to her parents, telling them that she was okay and that she loved them and especially sent her love to Rosemary. She did however, ask them not to contact her where she lived. Margaret then hurried over to Mrs. Wilson's. When she answered the door Margaret asked if she could please mail this short letter for her. She agreed and Margaret asked if she could put her return address on the letter so that if she received a reply it would first come to Mrs. Wilson's home. She agreed to do this and said she would give Margaret's family her phone number as well. Margaret was relieved and grateful that she never asked her any questions. She also didn't mention the bruises on her face or her swollen lip. She only said softly, "Dear, I am here for you if you need my help." In her heart Margaret thought, thank you God for small favors.

John did all the shopping for their food, telling Margaret what to cook and when to cook it. He also got bags of clothing for her at the Goodwill store. He told Margaret how to dress and then he told her how to braid her hair and wear it pinned up with the braids wrapped around her head. He also made her stop using lipstick. In his own sick way, he was turning Margaret into a woman who looked like his Mother. Margaret was so shocked by this abnormal behavior that she didn't even know anymore, if she wanted to live or die. One moment she wanted to survive and the next she thought she'd rather die. One day she caught a glimpse of herself as she passed by a mirror. She didn't know who she was looking at but this couldn't be her. She looked just like a woman from an old-folks home. This had become her pattern of living, if you'd call it living.

23
the recovery

When Margaret was alone she would pass the time daydreaming of the mountains and of nature. She would look out of the window and tried to see something of beauty. She also wrote letters to God in her journal, praying that there could somewhere be a God.

She realized now that the man she had married was a monster and when she disobeyed him he would look and act like a crazy mad man. One time in particular he kicked Margaret in the knee and she had to hobble around for two weeks, all this was just because, his coffee was late being perked! Another time he accused Margaret of hating him and said that she never smiled at him. He told her that he had picked her up and married her and gave her a nice home with food and clothing, and that he had bought her new teeth. He said, "You are ungrateful and lazy and I don't even know why I bother with you." Margaret didn't know how to answer him because she knew that she didn't want to provoke him into attacking her. So she tried to smile and thank him for his care. She became an actress and tried to be nice whenever he was around.

When Margaret would think back over all of the past years of her life she would wonder how all of this had happened to her. Why? Why did bad things keep coming her way? How different her life might have been if she had never been with Wyatt Kendall and hadn't fallen for Jim. Maybe she wouldn't have started drinking and being a prostitute. It was like a mud slide of her own doing. She thought that she had landed in her private one-woman hell with the devil as her jailer. *When will this misery ever end?* Before Margaret realized it, the tears would flow like a river, making her eyes red and swollen and all she can think of is *Please, God, please don't let John notice how I look or he will beat me for crying.*

Margaret finally fell asleep from exhaustion. She began dreaming that she was with her Grandma Boucher, her Mom's mother. She was about five years old at the time and Grandma held her close by her side as they sat on an old horsehair settee. She was reading to Margaret from her old worn black King James Bible, which she kept nearby at all times. She looked at her and said, "Margaret, Jesus is the answer for all of our needs, He loves us and protects us throughout our lives no matter what." Margaret thought, "Grandma, how can Jesus be the answer when we do wrong?" What she didn't tell Margaret was that we all have free will and that if we do something wrong then we must also pay by suffering the consequences. Then she remembered how she had always wanted to make her own decisions, even when she was a very young child. First she had chosen Howard, then after being hurt by him, she went right out into the arms of Wyatt Kendall. One mistake right after another.

She then remembered a Bible story that Grandma had read to her once about the prodigal Son who spent all of his money being bad but then when all of his money was gone he returned home to his father's house. He found that his father loved him and forgave him for all of the bad things that he had done. Slipping to her knees Margaret prayed, *Please heavenly Father forgive me and let me be a good person from this moment on.* She didn't know if God had heard her but she felt somewhat better about everything. Margaret thought, *where else can you go when you are in such deep despair.* She seemed to have a little more energy now. She scrubbed the floors of the apartment on her hands and knees and then washed and ironed the clothes them to keep busy. She tried to be thankful for a roof over her head. She thought, *at least I'm not in a dirty jail cell or being a bad woman anymore,* She didn't drink beer or wine now and she only wanted peace, knowing that her daughter was safe with her mother and dad.

Time passed and days ran into weeks, then weeks turned into years. Margaret seemed to accept her lot in life, unhappy as it was. John began drinking more and more and at times he fell asleep into his plate of food, not shaving for days at a time. Margaret thought that he did not beat her as much lately and she was grateful for that. With so much time spent alone with no human contact Margaret would find herself daydreaming and remembering about, Rosemary, back when she was just a tiny infant. She thought that she didn't get to enjoy her as much as she would have liked.

She remembered what a pretty baby she had been. Everyone, else in her family seemed to look on the baby with amazement at the perfection of her. Her hair was blonde with reddish highlights and the lashes around her big blue eyes were long and curled up. She smiled and clapped her hands and made us all notice her as she began to sit up and then crawl. When she took her first steps she went to Margaret's mother. These two had a special

connection from day one, from the very beginning. Oh..
how much her Mother had loved the child and Rosemary
seemed to   love all of Margaret's brothers and sisters
loving the attention they gave to her. Margaret's father
called her his little sweet angel. No matter how tired he
was when he came home from the back-breaking work in
the coal mines he never failed to hold her high above his
head and kiss her on both cheeks. Then he would laugh
and ask her how her day had been. She was the sunshine
in their dreary, everyday life. What a blessing Rosemary
had been to everyone despite the disgrace of how she was
conceived out of wedlock. She was so perfect; it was as if
she was born into the wrong family.

24
those mountain memories

John and Margaret did okay for about two weeks but one night he didn't come home. It was morning when he showed up looking like a dirty and unshaven bum off the street with the smell of liquor all over him.

"Are you alright?" she asked. He looked at me through bloodshot eyes and reached out his fist and hit me in the mouth. "Fix me something to eat, you lazy leach! You're good for nothing. I don't know how I got stuck with the likes of you?"

He hit her across her face and her lips swelled up and blood ran off her chin. All she could think was, *Thank God my new teeth were not broken. How could this keep happening to me?* She felt like she was in a nightmare. He ate the food she prepared and fell asleep on the couch. She just sat on the floor and cried until no more tears would fall. She found herself lonely and longing for something positive in her life to hold onto. Her thoughts began to wonder and she found herself dreaming once more about her childhood. Even though she was poor and grew up living in poverty, Margaret felt deep love for her family and cherished the fond memories they shared.

That night looking out at the full moon shining above the glistening white snow, Margaret prayed, *please God direct my life and help me to be pleasing to you.* She didn't have a deep faith in God, yet she still prayed to Him and it gave her comfort. The next morning he awoke and after washing and a cup of coffee, he cried, "I'm so sorry. I don't know what made me punch you? I go crazy sometimes but I promise never to hurt you again."

Margaret knew these were empty words. John had a Jekyll and Hyde personality and he was mentally sick and angry. She became the outlet for his sickness and found herself escaping reality. After all, when your world is a life of hell, you perhaps let yourself daydream, closing out the real world of fear, pain, disappointment and shame. That became Margaret's daily routine. She would let her mind wander to the days of her youth--recalling the mountains that rose up high almost crowding out the sky.

The Appalachian mountain range stood majestic and proud surrounding the hollow where she grew up. When she closed her eyes, she could almost smell the clean fresh air. She felt the wind blowing her hair around her face and the feel of the soft green grass against her feet in the summertime. That escape was the way Margaret coped with an abusive husband. She remembers the first time she fell in love with the mountain tops. Her parents had taken Margaret and her sister Macel up to visit her father's parents. Her grandparents lived in a shanty on the summit of the hill above their town. Her Grandpa had an old mule and a wagon and he made a living cutting trees from the forest. He would sell the lumber to the company store, that was owned by the coal company to build homes. They enjoyed the peace and solitude of living atop the mountain. They farmed and planted vegetables to feed themselves and to sustain them through the winter. They were very happy and content living in their simple lifestyle.

One day Margaret wandered to the edge of their property to look out with wonder at the vast space. Looking down at the trees, she could see a small stream that formed a waterfall below. She really loved the sights, the smell and the sounds of the mountain life. Her grandparents had lived and raised their family of six children in the coal mining town of Burnwell, just like her parents had lived and raised their children, until they were all gone from home. Grandpa built the shanty where he and his sweet wife, Margaret's Grandma lived happily enjoying life on the mountaintop and relished their life of peace. Grandpa used his old mule to haul the trees to make his living. Grandma sang songs and baked bread and worked the garden. The two of them were true soul mates and the happiness showed on their faces.

Grandma Betsy Weaver, her daddy's mother, died in her rocking chair one morning of a possible heart attack. Grandpa was left alone with enough memories to last him for two more years until death took him. He then joined with Grandma under the old oak tree in the cemetery, about a half-mile from their shanty. Margaret remembered fondly how they looked to her. He was a tall man with white hair and a white beard, with eyes of blue that twinkled when he laughed. His laughter was contagious and he knew how to tell funny jokes. Margaret began to smile, as she thought back at the many good times shared together, on that old porch. Grandpa had a large tummy, almost like Santa Claus. Grandma was a little woman, hardly five feet tall in her stocking feet. She wore her hair in two braids pinned on top of her head. Her hair was brown but had silver streaks at the sides and her beautiful brown eyes were framed with long lashes.

Margaret remembered her with her different colored aprons made from old flour sacks. She adorned them with brightly colored pockets made from left over quilt scraps. Margaret especially liked the apron with the red pockets. This was because it was worn mostly on the days when grandma baked yeast bread and some times ginger spice cookies. As Margaret closed her eyes, she could almost, smell the fresh loaves of homemade bread, lined up on the kitchen table and the aroma of the ginger spiced cookies. Grandma always let Margaret sample the first cookie. Oh, how special it made her feel. Margaret's memories of her grandparents and their shanty in the mountains would be in her heart forever. It was in her blood, her heritage, no matter where she went in life, no matter how many years passed she would always love and dream of living in the mountains.

Margaret recalled convincing one of her brothers or sisters to go with her and climb the winding dirt road, up to see Grandma and Grandpa. Whenever, she'd ask "please tell me a story" they laughed, looking at one another and smiling. "Margaret, why do you want to hear all about life long ago?" her siblings would ask. But then Grandma, wiping her hands on her apron, would sit down and in her southern accent start to pour out the beautiful love story that touched Margaret's heart. Grandma told about how she grew up in a town called Blooming Rose, about ninety miles away. She had two older sisters and her family owned a small farm but her Daddy had hard time farming so he moved the family to Burnwell. Grandpa started to work in the coal mines, everything was ugly there and the whole family was sad. The soot from the coal covered the roads and the houses. The houses were gray and poorly built to begin with and the soot only added to the ugliness.

All three of the girls started school in Burnwell and most of the children were nice enough to welcome them. Sitting next to Grandma in school was a boy named William. Little did she know that this shy boy would be her future husband. He had the sweetest smile and he studied very hard to learn his lessons. Back then when young boys turned fourteen they would begin to work in the mines. William knew he would have to quit school and work in the mines to help his family. He also had two older sisters, and Grandma's family gradually accepted living in Burnwell. The only social thing to do was to go to church, which they all did every Sunday. One night a month they would go to a square dance that was the only entertainment. When William had to quit school and begin working in the mines, Grandma missed seeing him in school. She later learned that he was too tired to even come to the square dances. She didn't get to see him only occasionally at church. The years passed and Grandma began to grow from a young lanky girl with long brown hair into a woman. She had hopes and dreams of meeting Mr. Right and moving far away from the coal mining life.

Her sisters had both moved away after their marriages. Grandma told that all the other girls in town had sweet hearts and went and danced on Saturday night, but not her. She thought she would be an old maid because she didn't like anyone around there. That's when out of the blue, a very handsome boy came to visit her one Sunday after church. At first she didn't recognize him, he was so tall and his shoulders were wide, but when he took off his hat and she looked into his eyes, to her amazement it was William. Talk about people changing, he was not a boy any longer, but a man. Grandma said her heart skipped a beat, she couldn't even speak and she just stared at him. He said, "Betsy, I've been very busy and a lot of things have occurred in my life, I've grown up I guess." Then he laughed and said, "The one thing I know is that you are the only girl for me. I can't get you out of my mind. Do you have a beau?" When she could speak, she answered, "No, not anyone." He asked, "Do you think I could call on you? Maybe go to church with you and visit in the evening?" Grandma said that her joy at that moment knew no bounds; in her heart on that very day she felt that he was to be her one true love. From then on they saw each other every Sunday and two months later William asked Grandma for her hand in marriage. Her parents were so happy for them that they gave their blessings. The only thing Grandma's parents asked was could they please live nearby. William agreed to this and the wedding was scheduled for one month later in a little church in Burnwell. Although their world in Burnwell was an ugly place, they were looking through the eyes of love. Betsy would sing as she helped her mother with plans for her wedding dress. It would be handmade by her mother but she would buy material from the company store instead of flour sacks that were used for most all of the everyday dresses.

Her mother wanted to provide the very best wedding dress for her. She made a hand crocheted bodice with tiny pearl buttons in the back and a skirt that graced the floor. Grandma recalled that she carried a bouquet of pink roses from the back fence, being so thankful that it was June. She said they had an old, wooden fence out in back of the house where they lived and roses bloomed every summer and entwined the wooden slats. Her mother had babied those pink climbing rose bushes every summer since they had moved there from the farm in Blooming Rose. They brought her great joy to see them bloom every summer. William had rented a house for them to live just down the road from Grandma's parents. It looked gray from the front like all the other houses but it was to be our own home. Grandma sewed curtains for the windows and tablecloths for the table. She was the happiest girl in the world to be William's bride. She recounted walking down the aisle toward him and felt like Cinderella and he was her Prince Charming.

25
regrets

Grandma and Grandpa had begun their lives over forty years ago. They had six wonderful children, Grandma said, they had been blessed. Then their dreams came true when they moved up the mountain to their shanty. There on the mountaintops they had received all that they could have dreamed of, love and happiness, good health and wonderful grandchildren. Margaret wondered why all girls couldn't be so blessed as Grandma. She had made so many bad choices: picked the wrong man, tried to run her own life instead of serving God and letting him guide her life. Every time she would think back on her life she'd wished things could have been different for her but in life you can never go back, only start anew trying to make things right. Now, thinking about her life with John, living like a prisoner and enduring his abuse, she knew that he had her locked into his life of misery. All she had left now is long ago memories and regrets.

Margaret's only concession was writing poems to God and letters to her family, when she could sneak one out to be mailed. In her diary she poured her heart to Rosemary and kept it hidden from John. Margaret recalled that she had been in this abusive relationship with John for ten long years. Looking back over her life she realized that she had failed miserably in many ways. She tried to live day by day, doing the best she could to take care of John and his needs. She knew that he was a sick man but that he refused to seek help. He just continued to drink and to hang out with the wrong kind of people. He seemed to be content with Margaret, as long as she was his prisoner, his cook and housekeeper.

John required that Margaret be silent and not complain about her life. She learned to obey him and the beatings would not come as often. Margaret relied on God to help her and she prayed daily for the strength to go on. One of the saddest days of Margaret's life was when she had learned that her daddy had been killed in a mining accident. He was too old to still work and this would have been his last year of work. A heavy piece of equipment had collapsed, killing five men died that day, including her father. Margaret recalled how John had also beaten her severely that day when she wanted to go to her Mother's side in her time of need but he would let her go. He stayed home for three days to guard her from leaving the house. He threatened her neighbor friend who gave her the letter with the news of her Father's death saying that he would blacken her eyes if she interfered with their business.

So, the only thing Margaret could do was the next best thing. She wrote a note of apology to her mother and had to sneak it to the mailbox, after John had finally gone out to the beer joint. Margaret knew that John was a monster and that he fooled her when they first met. He is an alcoholic and schizophrenic with a government pension. He was also her jailer and she had no way out of this life, except to dream herself into a different life full of hope. A place where Margaret would be able to smile and do nice things for people that she loves.

Margaret loved to look out of her window and see the sunshine, or at times catch a glimpse of a red robin looking for a worm. The things of nature had become so very precious to her. They were wondrous to her as a child and now even more as she had grown older. She thought how she would love to be free to walk at night and gaze at the stars and the big golden moon. To feel the sun on her face to perhaps walk in the soft, green grass again. Margaret was not allowed to ever go out of the door of their apartment. John had put the fear of death into her and she thought, *I am a coward, I guess I really have nowhere to go, no money, no way to earn a living.* He had convinced her that she was worthless. This is the way an abusive man controls his victim, through put downs, fears ,beatings and isolation. Margaret thought, *someday I will die and at last I will be free of him. Let it be, dear Lord,* she prayed. She'd grown weary of this life and really didn't want to go on much longer.

One day Margaret was looking out of the kitchen window located above the sink. She had just finished washing the breakfast dishes. John was leaving and as the door latch closed, her eye caught a sight on the windowsill. It was a caterpillar moving and twisting its way along and after a long while it emerged with wings. Margaret was startled to actually see a butterfly. How wonderful she thought, to see ugliness turn into a thing of beauty and it made her day. God's plan is to change life. Oh, how she wished He could change her. He had made her brand new on the inside and she believed He forgave her sins. She only wished He would change her outward circumstances.

She just had to be thankful for her blessings, she kept

telling herself. She had food and clothing and a warm place to live. She had her health and her daughter was also doing alright. At times, if she thought about it too much, she would weep over her past but then she would try to make the best of things. She would distract herself by writing a poem, or at other times, she would try to practice writing John's name on a piece of paper. She was afraid that John would catch her doing this but she was getting better at copying his signature. It was getting to look remarkably like his own writing. This was a crazy thing Margaret would do, to pass the many hours that she spent alone in the apartment. After she was through practicing writing John's signature, she would flush all the paper down the toilet. This was to keep him from ever finding out what she was able to do with his name.

Margaret never received any phone calls as everyone in her family had been told that she would get into trouble if John found out that she has had any contact with anyone. When the phone rang she was almost afraid to pick up the receiver. When she said "hello" and heard the voice she instinctively knew that it was to be bad news. It was her mother in tears informing Margaret that Rosemary had run away. Margaret almost fainted from the shock of the words. At the age of sixteen where could she have gone? She was in total disbelief, however, she tried to calm herself, and convince her mother, that Rosemary would be alright. "Please Mother, don't worry. I will find her. She will come see me...I am sure of that. I will call you as soon as I hear from her."

Almost immediately there was a knock at the door. There stood Rosemary. She hugged her mother tightly and sobbed out her tragic story. Margaret then called her mother to say that Rosemary was now safe with her. In a state of panic, Margaret also whispered a quick prayer to God for His help and for an answer of what to do in this situation! Then a final prayer of thanksgiving that her daughter was with her tonight. She was extremely grateful that John was out for the entire night. This was his poker night and he wouldn't be coming home until early tomorrow morning. She sat down with her daughter and the entire story came tumbling out. The words a mother never wants to hear. She cried bitter tears as Rosemary told her that she had been raped. Her young heart had been broken. Rosemary thought that he was a friend who had offered to take her home from one of the dances. She thought that she could trust him, but instead he took advantage of her.

The scene played over and over in Rosemary's mind... the way he ripped her clothing...the uncontrollable rage she saw in his eyes and the pain she felt when he penetrated her young body. *Dear God, please help me!* Rosemary began sobbing again, hardly able to speak. She had been violated and it made her feel cheap. She explained she never meant to run away and worry anyone but everyone knew that if Grandpa found out that Rosemary had been raped, he would have killed the boy. Margaret looked deep into Rosemary's eyes and felt her daughter's pain and angst. Margaret knew firsthand the feeling of her pain. However, this was far worse. This was *her* baby girl. Why hadn't she been there to protect her. A horrible feeling of guilt washed over her and she puzzled over what were they going to do?

26
cousin charles

Margaret tried to calm Rosemary down attempting to gain her own composure for her daughter's sake. Her mind raced with a collage of emotions ranging from elation at seeing Rosemary, to fear and despair as to what happened. Given the circumstances she knew that she had to act quickly and without hesitation. She turned to her older brother Russell for help. Russell had a son named Charles who lived in Cleveland, Ohio. Margaret had always been close to Russell and Charles. They had always been kind, compassionate and supportive to Margaret, even during the darkest moments of her life.

She knew she couldn't keep Rosemary there with her because of John. Margaret prayed to God to help her decide what to do. Margaret quickly decided a call to her Russell was the best thing to do. She hoped that John would not find out that she had used the phone. He would beat her if he found out, however, that was the last thing on her mind at the moment. Her daughter needed her and it was a risk that she was willing to take. She had to find a solution fast and Russell and Charles was her best hope.

As it happened, Charles, his wife Jean and their young daughter were visiting Russell for a week. After Margaret quickly blurted out her dilemma to Russell, he put Charles on the phone. Margaret tried to explain the situation to Charles and how it was impossible to have Rosemary there with her and John. Charles listened quietly to the distress in Margaret's voice. Then he said that he was leaving in the morning and that if Rosemary wanted to go with him and his family he would take her back to his home. They would help care for her as best that they could. Margaret was so relieved and thankful to Charles as this was truly the answer to her prayers. Rosemary agreed to go with them. Charles tried to convince Margaret to come with them as well but she had to refuse his offer. She remembered the deep dark secret that no one else in the whole world was aware of except John. One night during one of her recurring nightmares, John had learned of the awful crimes she had committed in her past. He had been holding this over her head with the constant threat of prison. Margaret knew her decision to not leave John and go with them had made them unhappy, but she had no choice. They thought she must be truly insane to live that way but she felt it was her only choice for now.

Russell and Cousin Charles wanted to help Margaret and Rosemary and *everyone* in her family wanted Margaret to leave John and his abusive and manipulative ways. They told her that she could run away with Rosemary be safe to start a new life with them. She wished with all her heart she could accept their generous offer and go. What nobody in her family understood was her distant past. It was to her undoing that John had heard her talking in her sleep about what she had done. He seemed so interested and so glad and made her tell him all about what her crimes were. John used this confession to keep Margaret imprisoned. He threatened to go to the police with the story if she ever tried to leave. She had to remain there, locked up with her own fear and regret.

Margaret felt her life was spiraling downward and she just kept sliding further down. She felt as though there was no way out for her. Margaret's mother had told her when she was a little girl that every cloud had a silver lining and she wondered when she was ever going to find hers. Only thoughts of her daughter and her safety brought joy and, if Rosemary could have a new beginning then she could endure this life, filled with sadness.

As Margaret looked out the window at the night sky, the moon was shining brightly and the stars were twinkling. She prayed for God to watch over them and recited the little poem, **Twinkle, Twinkle Little Star**. She reflected how different life was for her when she was a little girl and she had first learned this little song. She thought of how peaceful the world was when John was out all night. The house, with beautiful silence allowing to look out upon the wondrous night sky. She could not close her eyes on this particular night. She watched in wonder over her dear Rosemary as she slept; Margaret kept a vigil over her that night, savoring the sight of her dear daughter. She wished for Rosemary to have a wonderful life with a good husband and beautiful children to bless her. It was a life completely different from the hell Margaret now found herself living in. The sound of the clock ticking made Margaret realize the hours seemed to be passing by so quickly. She feared that John would decide to come home early and find Rosemary here with her and her heart began to beat fast. Her hands were clammy with sweat on her brow. She was so frightened that she could hear her blood pounding in her ears.

Yet, at the same time she felt the joy of looking upon the sweet figure of her daughter, whom she had not had the pleasure of seeing for almost an entire year. It was a bittersweet night.

Margaret prayed the rape would not leave lasting harm on daughter and begged God to not allow an unwanted pregnancy for Rosemary. Only time would tell what lay ahead for her and it was too horrible for her to even think about. She thought, *I must push it from my mind and try to think good thoughts.* Wringing her hands, she tried to keep herself from going insane. Margaret paced the floor all that night and revisited the turn of events that had happened to her daughter. Margaret had been through many years of suffering,from one bad thing after another, however, she knew that she had brought on so much of it herself. Rosemary was still a young girl and it broke her heart to see her only child suffer. Margaret's hands were tied as there wasn't much else that she could do. At least not while she lived in this prison with John.

She fearfully watched the door for John, listening for any sound of his early arrival. "Please God, "she prayed, "keep him away until I can safely get Rosemary on her way to Cleveland." She watched her daughter as she slept, wanting so much to hold her and keep her safe. She was truly the best thing, maybe the only good thing, to have happened to Margaret in her life. *If only I had been married when Rosemary was born,* she thought. Her daughter deserved a better life than she was able to provide for her. She prayed things would turn out alright for her being able to start life anew with her cousin's family.

The hours passed and, finally, it was time to awaken her daughter to say goodbye. How sad Margaret felt, though she was relieved to have been able to care for her daughter this one night without John finding out. She thanked God for this small blessing. Margaret woke Rosemary up, telling her that she must hurry to get ready to go with Charles to Cleveland. She told Rosemary, "You must be out of here before John comes home. He would be so mad to see someone here and you *don't* want to see him in a mad rage. I want you to be safe with Cousin Charles." She told Rosemary that it would be a new adventure for her in a big city, attempting to make it sound like a happy place for her to be. Margaret looked upon Rosemary and saw that her daughter had blossomed into a very pretty young woman yet she had experienced so much grief for one so young. Rosemary never truly experienced a real family. She had a mother who was unwed and troubled with a father had no interest in her whatsoever. Then to be molested by a so-called friend. *Please God, will it ever stop?* Margaret blamed herself because of the poor choices she had made. She hugged her daughter tight in her arms. Her heart was breaking as she kissed her daughter goodbye, not knowing when or if she would ever be with her again. Thinking of this she really began to weep bitterly. Only God could know how much she loved her daughter and only He could know how dearly she missed her. With all of her heart, she wished she could live with her, comfort her and help her to make her life good and whole. "Please God," she prayed, "Watch over her and help her to heal from this abuse, caused by that boy, who used her. Please help me find a way I can be free of this monster I married. I know that I've made so many mistakes but I want a better life".

The sound of a car horn interrupted Margaret's thoughts. She took a deep breath and proceeded to open the front door, seeing Cousin Charles and his wife Jean as they pulled up into the gravel driveway. Rosemary quickly gathered her bright red sweater and turned and hugged her mother. With tears flowing down both cheeks, Rosemary embraced her mother one last time.

Margaret's hands trembled and her heart cried out in angst as Rosemary kissed her quickly before leaving. "Wait!" Margaret shouted as Rosemary rushed to the door entrance. Margaret reached deep into her apron pocket and pulled out a small gold, heart-shaped locket. Inside was a baby picture of Rosemary. "This was given to me by Grandma Bousher and now I want you to have it. Keep this as a reminder that in I will always be with and that you are always in my heart." Rosemary knew how precious the gold locket was to her mother and realized at that moment just how deep her mother's love was for her. Rosemary reached out her hand and lovingly accepted the locket and left.

Margaret looked out the window and watched Rosemary disappear down the street, inside the car with Cousin Charles and his family.

27
cleveland, ohio

Rosemary had deep feelings about this turning point in her life. She thought to herself, *What a difference a day can make in a life. Things can never be the same for me. Because of making one mistake and trusting a man that I thought I knew. Now I am no longer a virgin.*

Now, I can no longer live with my grandparents. I must get into a car with my mother's cousin and his wife. I will be taken far away to a big city. I am going to start my life anew among people who are strangers to me. These thoughts were swirling around in her head, trying as she might to put a smile on her face for mother. She knew her mother had been up most of the night worried about what would happen to to her if she didn't go to Cleveland with her Cousin Charles and his family. So Rosemary said, "Mother this will be a great chance for me to get a job and maybe even a good education. Don't worry about me. I will be fine." Just then Cousin Charles' car pulled up in front of the apartment. The time to leave was now.

Gathering her few belongings, Rosemary rushed out

of the door. The tears were making her eyes so blurry she could hardly make out the faces of the very people who were offering her a home. Sitting back in the seat Rosemary mumbled a "Thank you" to the two of them. Once she was settled her thoughts returned to the events of the last few days. Rosemary was grateful that the small talk inside the car did not include her, as she wished only to be alone with her own thoughts. Finally these draining memories gave way to a deep sleep.

After many miles passed until the new, extended family stopped to have a meal, providing needed energy for another long stretch of driving. After an all-night driving session the sun began to rise. The warmth of this early morning sun woke Rosemary and after a hearty breakfast in a diner they began the final leg of the drive. After two more hours they arrived at their destination.

They greeted Rosemary to her new home with friendly, welcoming words and told her that it would be a safe haven for her. Rosemary thought that Cousin Charles' family seemed to be very nice people. She thought, *I just needed to get to know them. I need to forget about me and try to act grateful to be invited to share a room at their home. It's time to wipe away the tears and put on a happy face.* Rosemary looked all around her new surroundings. Her new life was about to begin, here in this big city in Ohio.

28
a letter from mother

Margaret watched the car drive away and she kept looking until it was out of her sight. Margaret wiped the tears away, *I must get control of myself.*

At least Rosemary was gone before John got home. Margaret finally had fallen to asleep after no more tears would come. She was awakened by the sound of John coming through the door. He barked, "Woman, I am hungry, are you too lazy to cook for me?" Margaret jumped to her feet and said, "I have some chicken cooked for you." She always tried to be prepared with food for John whenever he came home. Now looking at this man, she felt repulsed. His eyes were red and swollen, his hair was falling in his face and he was in need of a shave and a good bath. His clothing was wrinkled and the odor of stale beer filled the room. Margaret thought to herself how sad it was for a person to fall so far into sin. He had been up all night drinking booze and he was almost falling asleep in his plate of food. Margaret said, "John let me help you to get into bed". "Don't touch me" he yelled at her. Margaret backed away and let him sleep at the table. She was grateful for this time of quiet and peacefulness. She read her bible and tried to hold on to her faith in God. She prayed for a way to escape from this prison. She had placed her daughter into God's hands and she was thankful for Cousin Charles taking Rosemary home with him.

The lady next door knocked softly on the window glass. She said she didn't care to interfere but that Margaret's mother had written a letter to her and it had come to the her address. Margaret thanked her neighbor then, when she was alone again she quietly opened the envelope and began to read while John slept.

Dear Margaret,

I hope you get this letter as I sent it to your neighbor. She is very nice. I don't want to upset you. I know your life is hard and I so wish that I could help you. I wish that you could have had a good happy marriage. I don't know if I should tell you my news, but I will. Last month a man showed up at our door. He just stood there with his hat in his hands. He had his head bent. I didn't recognize him at first.

Then he asked for you. It was Wyatt Kendall. He looked much older but it has been a long time since I have seen him.

"What are you coming around here for, I blurted out. After all these years, you have the nerve. What do you want? My daughter is not here. State your business? Haven't you caused my daughter enough grief? What about your wife and kids?"

He just stood there and let me question him. That's when I noticed the tears in his eyes. He then began to tell me how he had changed. He said he was so sorry for the way he had hurt Margaret. He also said his family was doing well but that he could not forget the fact that you were pregnant when he left you.

He knew he had a child but drinking made him drown out

his conscience all these years. One day recently he went to church and asked God to forgive him for his sin. He came here to ask forgiveness from you. He said that he could not rest until he made things right with you and his daughter.

I almost felt sorry for him, Then I said, "Go home, Mr. Kendall. It's a little too late. My daughter and your daughter are out of your reach. Nothing could make up for the way you shamed them. As for the child that was born of your blood, she would only be hurt once more, it would be like tearing the scab off from a wound."

Wyatt said, "Please, I know I don't deserve forgiveness from you or from anyone in your family. I would do anything to ease the pain I have caused you all. The one thing I ask is if you could find it in your heart to allow Margaret and...my daughter to know that I am truly sorry. "

I was in shock by his visit. So many thoughts in my head. Can a person change? Can they make up for sins that hurt so many people? I know that God forgives and he really seemed to be sincere.

I wonder how little Rosemary would take this news?

Well, sweetheart, that's up to you whether you tell her about him or not. I don't want to add to your problems. I hope John is treating you better now that we all stay away from you. Your Father is still weak but we are holding onto each other. We just have to trust God. I will hope to get a letter from you if you can sneak one to your neighbor to mail for you. Please be safe and know that you are loved by all of your family.

Love,
Mom

Margaret tore the pages into small pieces not wanting anyone to read these words. How could that man have the gall to ask my mother about Rosemary and me. Margaret couldn't shut out the words of that letter. She tossed and turned in bed that night thinking of what a wonderful daughter had been born from her time spent with Wyatt Kendall. He had a wife and two children, a real life. How different from the life Rosemary and I have. Was it fair for him to change and come asking about Rosemary now? Is it fair, or right, to tell her? Maybe someday, but not now. She had too much to deal without adding her father to the mix. Margaret was grateful to God for providing her a secret friend in the neighbor. Margaret knew she could trust her to send a return letter to her mother.

Margaret wrote to her mother saying she was doing alright for now. God is good to me. About Wyatt Kendall she added, *I'm glad he has changed and I am trying to forgive him. I don't feel it's the right time to share this with Rosemary. Please take care of yourself, and know that I love all of my family.*

Love, Margaret

29
life with john

At times like this, Margaret wanted and needed to escape the moment. The world that she was trapped in with John was so horrible that she would often daydream of how she wished her life could be. First she would create in her mind, a paradise for herself and Rosemary to live in. Paradise means different things to different people. To some people it means a beautiful home with paint on the outside boards, a new car in the driveway with a lot of money in the bank. Someone else's idea of paradise might be the elusive fountain of youth, never to grow old. To others it could be a man or woman, a soul mate, to share a life with and grow old together. Still to some it could be life near the seashore, with the sights of the ocean and the sounds of the birds, with the sandy shores to walk and gather seashells.

Paradise to Margaret would always and forever be a high and lofty mountaintop. A place of majestic beauty overlooking deep valleys, where the air is clean and fresh and blissful solitude reigns. Where the songbirds sing and the eagle's soar far above the tree tops. This indeed was Margaret's dream of paradise. She was so drawn to the mountains, as a kitten is drawn to milk. Closing her eyes she could envision the beauty of a brilliant sun rising in the clear blue sky. Then she imagined the sunset with an array of reds and golds filling the sky. It was enough to take her breath away in the beautiful world in the mountains where her Grandpa's shanty sat. Daydreaming was her only escape...the only way that she was able to survive the absence of her daughter.

Margaret had grown used to her lonely existence. John had forbidden any contact with family members, including her daughter, which was the hardest part. She lived day-by-day trying to have faith in God and coping with a mentally deranged man. He came and went as he pleased; always making sure that she obeyed him. He was like a powder keg ready to explode if she crossed him in any way. Margaret thought that he actually enjoyed beating her, most of the time he would kick and hit her where the bruises wouldn't show. He would not allow her to make any noise or scream so the neighbors wouldn't hear her and if she did he would hurt her even more. She was forced to take the abuse in silence, sometimes praying that he would kill her though wanting to survive because she hoped hoping that one day she could get free from him, even if the chance was slim.

One day Margaret was alone when the phone rang. The sound startled her! She was hesitant to pick the receiver up afraid of what John would do to her this time if it was for her...or him. However, when the ringing persisted she gathered her courage and answered "Hello." She heard her sister Maddie's voice on the other end. She knew instinctively it must be bad news. Maddie was calling to tell Margaret that their mother had passed away after suffering a stroke. Now both of her parents were gone.

Margaret dropped the receiver and slipped to the floor, filled with deep sorrow. She had not seen anyone in her family for ten years. Her mother's death so soon after her daddy's was too much to bear. Margaret was finally able to find her voice and talk to her sister. Maddie said that their mom had not been well since losing their dad in a mining accident a year ago. Maddie said that her mother went peacefully and that their parents would now be reunited in Heaven. Margaret hung up after thanking her sister for calling her. Margaret didn't care if she did get beat up this time. Her heart hurt so much and she was full of grief. Margaret realized the special hurt and heartbreak of losing her parents. Her eyes were swollen and red when John came home but he was too drunk to even notice and she was grateful for that. He fell asleep after eating dinner and Margaret had her own time and space to grieve for her special parents, now both gone.

With the death of both parents and John's constant beatings, she finally reached the end of her rope. She wondered why it had taken her so long. John continued the beatings growing in their intensity. Making matters worse, two months after Rosemary went to live with her cousin, she received a phone call from Charles, informing her that Rosemary was pregnant and they placed her in a home for unwed mothers. They didn't want to tell Margaret because they knew she would worry, however, they assured her that she was well and doing fine. The thought of not being there for Rosemary caused her great anxiety and fear.

Months passed with no contact from Rosemary as her daughter was ashamed. Margaret poured out her love and understanding in a letter to Rosemary but there had been no reply. She reached a point of total collapse. She thought that finding a man to love and take care of all her needs would make her happy. She tried covering her guilt by drinking but that failed to work. She felt like such a hopeless case. It was then that she fell upon her knees and cried unto the Lord to please save her. The tears flowed like a river down her cheeks like a dam had broken. Still on the floor, as the tears subsided, she fell asleep. When she woke, she felt clean and peaceful. She knew God had heard her cry and she began to feel a glimmer of hope for the first time. She opened her Bible and read.

John's pattern of rage and violence worsened. First he would hit and then apologize and be remorseful. She could bear the pain from a broken bone but the emotional pain she endured was almost too much to bear. When she had first met him she thought life would be good, however she knew better now. He would give money to her then blame her for not having any money after he drank too much. He pawned his Marine Corp rings to get money to drink with then beat her up and mistreat her by cutting up the clothes he had bought for her the month before. She was thankful that he never hit her in the mouth and break her teeth.

One night she had a very special dream. In it she was together with her entire family and they were so happy. They were well dressed and no one was hungry. No one had a care in the world. Rosemary, her sweet daughter, was holding her hand. John was nowhere to be found. It was a wonderful, peaceful time. There was no sadness, depression or fear. She looked up to see Jesus smiling at her. He said, "Welcome home. Someday, all my children will enjoy heaven with me." Beautiful music surrounded her and angels with graceful wings were everywhere. Then she awoke and realized she had been sleeping. The dream provided a peaceful hope deep inside her heart.

She prayed daily for God to watch over her daughter and thanked Him for helping Rosemary to get through the trauma she had suffered from being raped and the pregnancy. She wished a better life for Rosemary than she had and she knew that God's guidance would help her to make the right choices to make that happen.

30

continued abuse

The letter came a day after Christmas. It was wrinkled as though it might have been wet. After Margaret read it a second time she realized the wetness was from tears...her daughter's tears. She was telling me she was pregnant.

She was living at a home for unwed mothers. Though Margaret had been told of her condition by Cousin Charles this was the first time Rosemary, herself, had written to her. Her daughter's heart was breaking and she felt her pain. She would have gladly taken Rosemary's pain away but all she could do was weep and pray for her.

Rosemary had said in the letter that ten other girls lived at the home and she was doing okay. She had food and a warm bed to sleep in. She also had good doctor's care.

They held church on Sundays for the girls and she had started to attend. She was asking God to forgive her but she also needed Margaret to forgive her. If Rosemary only knew how much she was loved then Rosemary would know her mother could never condemn her. She was her precious girl.

With John off on his daily drinking spree, Margaret found herself alone for many hours and her mind wandered, pondering the past and the numerous mistakes she had made. If only she could turn back the clock and start anew. She wished, most of all, that she could change the fateful day when, feeling desperate, she had sold herself for money. As the memory began to play, a fresh stream of tears ran down her cheeks.

It had been a cold day in December. Christmas was just around the corner. Her rent was due and she wanted to buy at least one small Christmas present for Rosemary. Though there was little work available, Margaret walked the lonely streets all morning attempting to find a job. Every restaurant and beer joint turned her away. She knew how badly she looked pretty. Her clothes were shabby and her shoes had very little heel left. Her hair was a stringy, dirty mess and helped accentuate the harsh lines now visible on her face from the years of drinking and abuse.

She was at a desperate crossroad of her life. She had to make a decision which path to take. One led her back to her parent's house. Looking back, she wished that she would have gone back to her family. The other path, however, called to her and unfortunately, desperately wanting to make it on her own, she followed willingly. She took her last quarter and stopped for a cup of coffee at a diner.

That's when she noticed him. He was a tall man with a full grey head of hair and beard. His hair was He looked like a kind man of about fifty years old who was sitting alone. He wore a brown, wool coat over a flannel, blue shirt with faded overalls and well-worn work boots that completed his outfit. He smiled at her and asked if she lived around there. They started to talk and she told him she had been out looking for work with no luck. He offered to buy her something to eat. She was so hungry and the food smelled good. She thanked him and he ordered a hot dog for her. He then asked if she would like to spend some time with him. He worked for the railroad and just arrived from Ohio. He was lonely and didn't know anyone locally. After about an hour of spending time together, eating and talking, he asked her to go to his hotel room. He said there was fifty dollars in it for her to show him a good time. He said no one would know about it and that he desperately needed the company of a woman.

Tears continued flowing as the events played in her mind like an old movie. *Why didn't she run away?* She had felt trapped wanting to provide for her daughter and herself. *At times, sin looks so good and seems to be the only way. She went with him that afternoon. When she left the hotel with the money in her pocket she felt this must have been the way Judas felt after he had betrayed Jesus his Lord. She felt that everyone who looked her way knew her dirty secret and saw her shame. Her hands were shook as she went into the drugstore and bought a bottle of wine.*

The memories overwhelmed her. Sinking to her knees she begin to pray, needing to calm her nerves and also her guilt. *"Please, God, I know you have forgiven me, but the awful memories continue to haunt me and torture me. I need to let them go and think of the one good thing in my life...my sweet Rosemary."*

Margaret reminisced about Rosemary's birth "How sweet and soft she had been, as a baby. Her little hands and feet made me laugh as I put lotion on them after her bath. The eyes that look at me as she nursed seemed to say "You're a good mommy, just hold me and let's be together." Just a few moments of thinking of Rosemary helped her to quit crying over her sins. Reality returned and reminded what her fate would be if she did not get busy cooking dinner for John. The smell of food seems to calm him down after he had been out drinking. Maybe a full stomach will cause him to fall asleep and she could survive another night without a beating. Just two weeks ago he busted her mouth and the swelling of her lips had finally subsided.

She truly lived a life of hell with him. She was fearful and responded quickly at his beck and call. The only thing good was that she knew Jesus had forgiven her-- even if she could not forgive herself. She surmised that death would be a relief, but she knew she was too much of a coward to take her own life. Deep down there was a little seed of desire to one day, somehow, be with her sweet girl and live near the closeness of her family. She didn't know how this could ever come about but she held onto this hope, pouring out her love for Rosemary in her little diary. She then hid it away under the floorboards in the kitchen cupboard never wanting John to find it. He would tear it up into pieces and laugh at her while she cried.

John bought the food from the grocery store and even the clothes he required her to wear. Going to Church was out of the question. He didn't allow her to speak to anyone. God became her only companion and friend. She hid her Bible away when he came home because she feared that he would take that from her as well, leaving her completely alone.

The first time she endured beating happened several years ago from another man. She had not yet met John. It was a stranger that knocked out her two front teeth and blackened her eyes. She felt that was the worst time of her life at the time, however, John's constant abuse far exceeded that one instance.

It usually began with a cuss word and accusations of never cooking the food that he liked to eat. She cooked every day to try and please him. This night was somehow different. He slammed the door and called her name. "Margaret, where are you?" She came in from the back yard where she had put out a bag of trash in the waste can. He had lost all his money playing poker and had been out drinking all night. He said to her, "You are a lazy, good-for-nothing woman!" John then pushed her hard, crushing her backbone against a dresser drawer. She heard a sharp crack and fell to the floor. The pain her and she was unable to move. "Please John, stop! My back! I think my back is broken!" she cried.

Suddenly, his expression changed and remorse set-in. He said "I'm sorry, I didn't mean to hurt you." Lifting her, he laid her on the bed and went to a neighbor's for help. With the neighbor's help they went to the hospital.

She could not walk or bear any weight. The x-rays showed broken vertebrae in her lower spine. She was in traction for two weeks. She was then given pain pills and a steel brace to wear. This allowed her to be released from the hospital. John promised that he would never hurt her again. For a short period of time he was better and he even helped her around the house.

The doctor said she could try not wearing a brace after a month and to be careful with her activities. It seemed like the moment the brace came off, the beatings resumed. John began to drink again and staying out like before. This time he beat her in places where it would not show on her body. He started to whip her with his belt to punish her. As she felt the leather hit her body and heard the crack Margaret cried out, "Please don't start again! Please!" When John had finished his session of punishment, Rosemary slowly rose and told him he would feel better if he rested and she would make him dinner. "Rest here," and she pointed to her chair, "I'll fix you something to eat."

"There's never any food to eat in this house!" ranted John. "All you ever do is read that Bible!" He grabbed it from her hand and tossed it across the room.

She moved swiftly toward the kitchen. She wanted

him to quiet down hoping to avoid any further scene. "Now, please don't be mad, just rest awhile." She rushed to warm some leftover chicken. Her hands shook as she put some biscuits in the oven to bake. As she turned around, she felt relieved to hear John snoring, asleep in her chair. *Peace at last*, she thought and looked down at him. He looked so badly in disarray and lost. She once wished she could help him but how can you help someone who doesn't feel they need help? Margaret began to sing a little song as she did her ironing and scrubbing clothes. Work is good for a person and thought how better she slept after working extra hard.

John stayed out late most of the time playing cards and drinking with his so-called friends. She didn't care what happened to her, but she often prayed for Rosemary. "Dear God, watch over my daughter. Please keep her safe." At times she would be in total despair as she would think back over all her years and wonder how she had gone from bad to worse. She could not blame anyone but herself. First of all, she wasn't saying that she was sorry for having her daughter--only sorry for the sin that was committed in the way she had been conceived. She was sorry for many things that she brought disgrace to her family. She had to get her mind off all these problems, as it often made her feel like she was going crazy. Her diary lay on the bedside table and she decided to relieve her mind from some of her heartache by writing poems.

31
rosemary's story

While Margaret, Rosemary's mother, was living with John, Rosemary was off living own life. It was a long story from the time she was fourteen, a homeless teenager to a grown-up woman. It was to be many years on a roller coaster ride. Once she got on, it went very fast and she couldn't seem to get off. Finally her feet were planted on solid ground. Rosemary thought, how wonderful it would be to go back and start life over but you never can. Rosemary remembered back to her early years.

She found herself singing in the kitchen and as she works around the Grandma close to her. At fourteen years of age, she was then living with her grandparents. Rosemary's mother had left her with her Grandma and Grandpa and rode away on a bus. She felt sad at her mother leaving her, but yet, she was happy for most of her life. She had been very close to her Grandma but knew she would miss Mother and her new friend, Mrs. Jamison. They had become very good friends even though she was as old as her Grandma. They shared a lot of stories and had a lot of fun times together. Many hours, while her mother was at work or had been out drinking, Rosemary found comfort with Mrs. Jamison. Wanting so much to help this child, whom she felt compassion and concern tried to teach her to write stories. She had also taught her to write some of the details of her life in a journal. This had been fun and one day when she grew up, she would share the journal with her own children. Rosemary felt sad as she watched Grandma wiping tears away from Mother's face as she left us. Rosemary knew that Grandma worried about her daughter Margaret, and she did too. However, she was really enjoying living in Blooming Rose, where she now resided.

They bathed in a washtub and when she would use it, her knees almost came up to her chin when sitting in the water. Bathing like this is kind of awkward, but to Rosemary it was worth it all just to be away from the city of Charleston. Rosemary ran barefoot everywhere she went except to church on Sunday. Rosemary also liked to help pick tomatoes and corn from the garden. The vegetables were so fresh and the food was so good. Her Grandma baked cornbread every day to go with the large pot of freshly cooked pinto beans. She also made delicious coleslaw from green onions and cabbage retrieved from the garden early that morning. All of Rosemary's aunts and uncles had moved away, and so she is the only one living with Grandma and Grandpa. Rosemary felt extra special. and her Grandma sang songs to God as she cooked. Grandpa still worked in a strip mine and got real dirty. He looked so tired when he came home from his job.

It is summer time now and school is out, but Rosemary is to stay here and go to school in the fall. Last night, a little black kitten came crying at their door. It was so cute. Rosemary asked Grandma if she could please keep it. The next morning, Grandma and Rosemary went looking for its mother. They checked all over the hollow, however, no one knew about the little black kitten or where it may have came from. Grandma had determined that the little kitten was a female and by its size, was probably about six weeks old. Animals were meant to live outside and not in the house and Rosemary was told that she could feed it and play with it until someone else claimed it. Her new joy was that little kitten.

She found some old rags and put them in a basket to make a small bed. She petted the little kitten, so much, that you would think the kitten's fur would be rubbed off. Rosemary laughed as her little friend licked her face and she named her Suzy.

One morning after Grandpa went to work, Grandma fixed a wonderful breakfast of biscuits, sausage and gravy. It was so good. "Thank you," she said as she hugged her Grandma. Grandma said, "I have something to show you. She opened the cedar chest and it smelled of lavender. The chest was a gift given to her grandma when she was fifteen. They called it a Hope Chest. There, on top of some folded up quilts, was a blue quilt with little white flowers in four-inch squares. Grandma and her mother had made it when her mother was a young girl. Grandma gave it to her and said, "This is for you, Rosemary. Put it on your bed." She felt so happy and ran to Grandma and said, "I love you and Grandpa so very much. I love my Mother too." Rosemary was learning to embroider a sampler and she wanted to give it to her sweet Grandma. It was about twelve inches high and read 'The Lord is my Shepherd, I shall not want.' Grandma was so proud that Rosemary had stitched it for her. She liked this gift that Rosemary had made it all by herself.

32
an unfortunate incident

The summer was passing fast and Rosemary knew that she would start school the first week in September. A school bus would be picking her up by the side of the road. Rosemary looked forward to having children her own age to play with and learning about history. History was her favorite subject and during the summer, a spinster schoolteacher had given her a used book on the Civil War. Even though the book was musty and tattered and torn beyond repair, she cherished it and read it every day. She had memorized things like the Gettysburg Address by Abraham Lincoln and she couldn't wait to recite it to the other children and her new teacher. Rosemary thought how she wanted to grow up and be a happy person, not sad like her Mother. She never wanted to drink alcohol or get drunk but wanted to be more like her Grandma. Even though her Grandma was pretty old, with grey hair and lines on her face, her eyes sparkled and her face lit up when she spoke of the goodness of God.

Grandpa was a man of few words. He had a straight

razor that he strapped on a long black strip of leather. He brushed shaving cream on his face and used the straight razor to shave it all off. Rosemary recalled how she was so glad that she was a girl and she didn't have to shave like a man. Her poor Grandpa was all stooped over from working in the coal mines for thirty years. He had a bad cough and that kept him up a lot at night. He was only fifty-five – but working in the coal mines in such harsh conditions made him feel and look much older.

Rosemary shared her every thought with Grandma. When she showed her Grandma her journal that she had started wto write with Mrs. Jones, Grandma said, "Rosemary, you are a natural story teller. Maybe someday you will write a book." Sometimes they would sit on the porch after supper. They would swing in the old country swing and Grandma would tell Rosemary about a time when she was young. It's hard for her to imagine about her Grandma or Grandpa ever being young. The sheer thought of it made her laugh; however, they were nice people and very good to her. She listened intently as her Grandma told one story after another of her childhood and her courtship with Grandpa.

Rosemary knew it was probably difficult for them to have a fourteen-year-old girl come to live with them. They had already raised their own ten children. She tried her best to listen to them and to obey their rules. Although she would have loved bringing the little kitten into their home, Rosemary obeyed the rules. She would of loved to have the soft little animal sleep with her but back in those days' people didn't want pets to be house guests. Rosemary's job was to carry water to their house. Every day she would take two buckets and go to the well, which was about two hundred yards away, and draw water from deep down inside. She would take the water home where it was used for cooking and drinking. A bucket with a dipper sat on their back porch railing to keep cool for drinking.

For the very first time in her life, Rosemary felt so special to have a bed all to herself. She could roll around as much as she wanted and not touch anyone. Rosemary remembered that there were so many children up here in this little town. That is if you can call this little place a town at all. In the center of Burnwell was a small post office and a grocery store. The Church of Christ stood near the end of town and about a mile up the road was the Baptist Church.

There was also a place on the side of the road where you could buy a soda pop and a hot dog. It had a small room where a jukebox played music when you put in a nickel. Some children went there on Saturdays to dance the jitterbug and listen to Elvis Presley sing *Hound Dog* and *Blue Suede Shoes*. This was a hangout for kids about fourteen to eighteen years of age. Rosemary had gone a few times on Saturday.

Rosemary had met four nice girls her age and two boys. Most of them went to her school and church. It was such fun to listen to the music. One Saturday evening one of the boys said he knew her Grandparents. He asked if she wanted to ride home with him because it might rain and he had an old car. Everyone else piled into someone else's old van and drove off. So she said she guessed she would ride along with him. It was getting late and she was always home before dark and she didn't want to worry Grandma. He drove past the turn off to her street and she said, "You passed the road where I live."

He said he was going just a bit further and then he would turn around. He had the radio on and music was playing Elvis. He turned off the road into a dark place with no houses which made Rosemary quite apprehensive. He pulled her close to him and said that he really liked her and tried to kiss her. She had never been kissed before and she pulled away. He pushed her back into the seat and held her with one hand and started to pull her underwear off. The material tore and she started to fight him but he was too strong, Rosemary was no match for him, he overpowered her and before she knew what was happening, he had unzipped his pants and fell on top of her pushing her down. He raped her and she screamed, but there was no one around to hear her. She pleaded with him to let her go but it happened so fast.

After he was done, he said, "You'd better not tell anyone about this. I could really hurt you or your family." Rosemary was devastated and scared beyond belief. She never wanted to be like her Mother. She had hopes and dreams of being a good girl—saving herself for the man she would marry. He pulled up to her house and let her out. "You better keep quiet about this!" he again threatened as he drove off. She was left there with tears streaming down her face and shivering from fear. She wiped her tears away and tried to put her clothes back in order. She prayed, "Please, dear God, don't let Grandma or Grandpa be able to tell that I've been hurt."

She forced a smile and said, "Sorry I'm late…it's because of the rain storm. I'm very tired and need to go to bed now. Good night, I'll see you in the morning."

There was blood on her clothes and Rosemary didn't want Grandma to see it or to see how upset she was. She paced the floor and listened and waited for them to turn off their lights and go to sleep. She wondered, *what am I going to do? Dear God, help me. Grandpa will kill the boy who did this to me as sure as I have a breath. I can't bring all this trouble down on my Grandparents. That is the law of the jungle …to protect your family. It's what every man should do. I've heard grandpa speak so often about this with grandma. He really regretted that my so-called father got away with shaming our family.*

Rosemary knew her Grandpa cared for all his family and she knew that he had a lot of love for her. He welcomed her to live with them and sometimes he would slip her a few coins and tell her not to tell Grandma. She watched as he cleaned and polished the guns that were on the wall in the backroom. His Grandfather had handed them down to him. Men in his family held old guns as special treasures. Though Rosemary never had a father she knew her Grandpa would always protect her just as if she was his own little girl. Years ago some of his family had even fought in feuds using these very guns. Now Rosemary knew he was a gentleman, not the type to go looking to take the gun against another. He would only fight to save a family member. If any one of them were harmed, he would be willing to kill or to die or whatever needed to be done, and the thought of this scared Rosemary.

Grandma said he was a man of honor just like all of his proud family before him. He started drinking a lot after Rosemary's mother got pregnant with her. He wanted to go after the man that was responsible but Grandma begged him to remember that all of his own family would go hungry if he went to jail and so he withdrew into himself and suffered in silence. "No one had better hurt anyone else in this family or I swear I will commit murder!" Those words echoed in Rosemary's mind as she wondered what she was going to do.

It seemed like it took forever for the house to grow quiet. She put a few belongings into a bag as she knew she must leave. She had saved up a few dollars for bus fare to Charleston. Her heart was beating so fast and she was so afraid that the least little noise would wake Grandma up. She unlatched the door and slipped out into the night.

The moon was big and stars were shining in the sky.

Everything seemed to be peaceful and quiet as if nothing had happened. Rosemary's world had just been turned upside down. *She needed to get away!* She just couldn't bring this grief down upon them. She left a note telling her Grandparents that she was going back to live with her mother. She loved Grandma and Grandpa so much but her mother needed her. This was a lie but she felt the truth would hurt them even more. At daylight she walked about a mile down the road and waited for a bus to come along. She was frightened but in despair. She had no other choice but to go to her Mother. She had only met John one time and didn't like him. He had bulging eyes and didn't smile much. She heard Grandma say her mother had problems since she had been married to him but she didn't go into detail about anything. Rosemary was growing up and most girls her age went to work or got married. She wanted to go to school and have a better life than her mother had, but now all that had changed in one day.

Rosemary got on the bus and was still tired. She was talking to herself, thinking, that at sixteen, she's a woman and maybe she could get a job at the dime store. She was very afraid and never had she been so lonely. She thought, *Where was my life going?* She was like a tumbleweed with no roots. People on the bus looked at her then turned away. She guessed they had their own problems.

33

the new arrival

Finally it was daybreak and Rosemary walked to the apartment where her mother lived with John, hoping he was not at home. She desperately needed to see her mother. She knocked on her door and waited for it to open. Then Rosemary fell into Margaret's arms--spilling out the whole incident between sobs. One minute she was a woman and the next just a baby wanting to be held in her mother's arms. After a warm bath and sleeping for a while, she felt a little better.

Her cousin, Charles and his wife came to see Rosemary and said they would love to have her come to Cleveland and live with them. Mother said this was the best for her, as John would never allow her to live with them. So off she went on a big adventure far away to an even larger city in Ohio. She got a job in the five and dime store and lived with her cousin Charles and his wife for a few months. Then she moved to the home for unwed girls where she met a girl named Mary Lou, who was a few years older than her. Rosemary was only sixteen and

Mary Lou was about twenty.

This girl wanted her to meet a friend of her boyfriend and since she had never had a boyfriend, she agreed. His name was Ted and he was very nice. They dated for about three months and they had kissed a few times but that was all. He treated her respectfully and life seemed to be good. Rosemary's girlfriend Mary Lou, also had a boyfriend that was cute. Mary Lou always said that he was tall, dark and handsome. The four of them went dancing and ate at a drive-in restaurant. Rosemary went shopping and bought some new clothes and felt on top of the world.

Rosemary would often think of her mother and she missed her grandparents terribly. She would push away the sadness. At seventeen she began living with Ted. He said they would get married after he turned twenty-one in six months. He talked her into believing it wasn't wrong to live together without the benefit of marriage. He said that sin was old-fashioned and that church was for old people.

Rosemary went back to West Virginia on a bus to get permission from her mother to marry Ted. In those days a girl under eighteen had to have a written statements from their parents to get married. Mother was so happy to see her and said that she looked all grown up. While she was there, Ted phoned and told her he had changed his mind about marrying her. He said he did not want her to come back and that his home was no longer hers. Rosemary was devastated, hurt and betrayed.

Rosemary knew she had to go back to Cleveland as she had no choice and nowhere else to go. Rosemary missed her period and began being sick to her stomach. Her friend, who lived next door to her Mother, took Rosemary to the hospital and could not believe that she was pregnant. She knew she had to get away from her mother before she found out about her condition. After all, her mother had her own problems. Her mother's life was a living Hell with that abusive man, John. Rosemary had her suspicions that he beat her up. Her Mother tried to hide her bruises from her, but she couldn't hide the fear in her eyes. Back to Cleveland, on a bus she went and this time she wept as people tried not to notice her.

When Rosemary arrived back in Cleveland she had to decide what she could do. Six months ago she and Ted had a small accident while driving a car. They were hit in the rear but no one was hurt. So she got off of the bus and went to see Ted's lawyer. She told him that her back was hurt from the car wreck. He gave her $200 to not sue him in court. She then went to see Ted and told him she was pregnant. He could only say that he was sorry, but alas he had found someone else.

Rosemary found a little room to rent and she felt that somehow she would survive without letting her family know of her condition. She did tell Cousin Charles and he cried and said he was sorry and partly to blame. Shortly after, Rosemary was so sick with a kidney infection that she went to see a doctor. She was taken into Booth Memorial Hospital, a hospital with one entire floor that was devoted to be a home for unwed girls. There were four small beds in each ward. "How did I end up here?" Rosemary thought. She remembered Grandma had said one time that sin passed from one generation to the next and now she guessed that Grandma was right. There were thirty to forty pregnant girls in the home and a depressing place to be .

Back then every girl there had her own sad story to tell. Most of them wanted to be good girls and had come there from far away places in order to hide their condition as pregnancy outside of marriage was a big disgrace. They would go back home after giving their babies away for adoption and some of them worked in the laundry of the hospital to help earn our keep. They would fold baby clothes, sheets and blankets. The Salvation Army helped support this home for unwed mothers and put on a church service every Sunday. Some ladies came in and tried to teach us how to crochet and knit. Rosemary thought, *here I am at barely eighteen years of age and I'm eight months pregnant.* She had no husband and no home to go home to. *How could this have happened to her,* she thought. *Why,* she wondered *do so many people's lives continue in a vicious cycle?* First, her mother had her outside of marriage, and then here she is, also pregnant with no husband. Rosemary wanted a better life but looking back she realized she had made many poor decisions in her young life. She thought, *What I should have done was not to have slept with Ted without the benefit of marriage. Grandma would be so ashamed of me. My own Mother is living with that terrible man, John. She is living in her own prison.* Rosemary learned a new word today. One of her roommates was telling them all about fabrication. How it was different from telling a lie because to fabricate means to tell a story that you wished to be true. It could possibly be true, so you pretend it to be so.

Rosemary ran to be alone and took her paper and pencil and started a letter to her dear sweet mother. It would be worth everything to her if I could tell her a story that would ease her worry about me. Oh how she wished this fabrication could be true.

Dear Mother, she wrote, *Guess what? I met a wonderful man here. We were both in church and we talked and liked each other immediately. He told me his first wife had died and he was so lonely. He said he owned a nice home and had a good job. He said he understands how a girl can get into trouble like I did. He asked me to marry him and he would adopt my baby.*

Rosemary thought, how wonderful it would be if things could happen like this. The baby was born a week ago. Mother, you have a grandson. I named him Robert. I really love my baby and want to be a good Mom like you and Grandma were to me. I am getting married in a month at a little Baptist church. So now you don't have to worry about me any longer. Some day soon I will send you some pictures.

Your loving daughter, Rosemary

Rosemary felt good after she mailed that letter to her Mother. It felt as though a load had been lifted from her shoulders. For her mother's sake Rosemary had invented this fabrication. Ted was now married and Rosemary and her baby were alone in the world. Her cousin Charles had said she could stay with him for six weeks. Rosemary wondered, *"Where is my prince charming?"* She thought, I guess that's why girls like me get into so much sin because they will believe anything a man says ,when he tells them they are pretty.

Rosemary thought that she was always looking for someone to love her. *Please, God, help me to somehow be able to keep my baby. Help me provide a home for us. This is a big world for a young girl with a baby. I know it is my fault but I want to make things better now.*

She wrapped her arms around her sweet little baby as they rode off on a Greyhound bus. She squeezed him close and prayed that God would help them both.

The baby was sleeping with his little head on her breast. She listened to his quiet breathing. She sat there and thought of this poem just for him.

My dear little boy, from this day forward I give you my heart. I will always love you and never want us to part. When you are grown up and remember your Mom, you'll know that you have been my blessing right from the start. I know it might sound corny, but I just love you so much.

At that he moved and looked into Rosemary's eyes as if to say "It's okay, Mom. I love you too." In her heart Rosemary pledged to care and protect her child with all of her strength. She knew she only had an eighth grade education, and the only work available was in a restaurant. There were no such things as Aid to Dependent Children back then. There were no disposable diapers and bottles. The baby bottles had to be sterilized and the formula mixed. No one told her she could breast feed her baby. Rosemary was so naive; she didn't even realize it was a possibility.

She thought that Ted was a nice man, but maybe he too only wanted to use me? She was so dumb. Rosemary thought that if she could just get married, maybe she could have a normal life. She never had a father, a brother or a sister. Her Mother was always so sad when Rosemary was a small child. Then, with all the drinking she went through, her life was so unhappy. And then worst of all she married John, a man who kept her in his prison and away from all her family.

Rosemary remembered fondly, the best time of her life, it was the two years she lived with her Grandparents. She was so happy then, so content, the most normal life she had ever had. That got all messed up because of the rape. She couldn't take the chance of her Grandpa committing murder, so she thought she'd run away and make her own way in life.

She remembered when she went to church with Grandma, she listened to the preaching but she never became a Christian. Rosemary wanted to live her life, her own way…to have fun and someday she might even become a movie star. She would surely marry Prince Charming and live happily ever after.

As she looked back now, she realized it was the wrong

way to think. She shouldn't have lived with Ted. He lied to her and it was a sin to live together outside of marriage. She was so ashamed of herself. Then she thought, here I am, here in a home for unwed mothers and about six months pregnant. The baby began moving inside her and it made her realize that it was real; it was a baby, not just a mistake. She was homeless and a disgrace just like my Mother had been.

Around her, there were about twenty other pregnant girls at the home, all from different states. Many would hide there until their babies were born and given up for adoption. They would go home broken hearted and pretend that it never happened. The months passed slowly. Rosemary learned to knit booties and she attended church services. One time when she had talked to Ted, he agreed to send her ten dollars a week until she had the baby. It gave her a little spending money. Some of the girls and Rosemary would go to the soda fountain once a week. They would treat themselves to a Coke or French fries. Rosemary also bought herself some stationery to write letters. But she is so ashamed to write to her family.

Rosemary's, Aunt Maxine could never have a baby. She was married and had a nice home and a husband. Rosemary did write to her and told her about her condition and the impending arrival of the baby. She also told her that she would allow her to adopt her baby. Aunt Maxine seemed happy and wanted this to happen.

Finally it was Rosemary's time, she had begun to go into labor. The contractions began and the pain was so intense that she would have died at the moment, if she had a choice. She was all-alone with no one to comfort or console her, and after twenty-four hours of labor pain, Rosemary felt like she was on the edge of insanity. Then, it finally happened, Rosemary gave birth to a baby that weighed eight pounds and nine ounces! By this time

Rosemary was in a state of total exhaustion. The next morning they brought the baby to her and she held him for the very first time. That was it, he was hers and she fell in love with him instantly as she held him to her breast. \ The nurse came into her room and said that she had a telephone call. It was Ted, but it wasn't good news or congratulations that he was calling with, he had called to let Rosemary know that he had just gotten married. What a contrast...a new wonderful baby and the father calls to say he had married someone else. Rosemary thought miserably, *Why is my life so much like my Mother's?*

Now Rosemary felt as though she was truly all alone in the world with a new baby. She named the baby Robert Eugene; he was like a precious flower.

A FLOWER

Oh, little flower upon your bed
Showing forth color so bright,
without a sound you bloom.
Just being what you were created to be,
a delight for eyes to see.
My little one I love you.
I wish I could hold you on my lap
next to my heart all the days of your life.
But I must let you go, to grow and to bloom;
to show forth your color and fragrance.
You are a beautiful flower in my life
given by God as a delight for my soul

Rosemary

Rosemary knew then, that she couldn't possibly give him away to her Aunt Maxine. She didn't know how she was going to care for him, she was homeless with this new baby, and she had no money or anyone to turn to. She despaired how she could provide a life for them both. There was no aid to dependent children then. She would somehow have to work and find someone to care for the baby while she was working. How dumb she felt, she had no experience being a new Mother and there was no one to show her to be one. She didn't even know you could breast feed a new baby, let alone how to do it, so formula had to be mixed and bottles had to be sterilized. There were no disposable bottles or diapers to make life easier on new Moms back then.

Rosemary's cousin Charles allowed her and the baby to come live with him for six weeks. She worked in a restaurant from midnight to morning and she slept during the day. Charles' wife cared for her newborn baby. The six weeks was a real hardship on them and their family, so when the six weeks was up they put Rosemary and her baby on a bus and sent them away.

Rosemary had an eighth-grade education and no where to go with a newborn baby. Her Aunt Maxine allowed her to come to her house to make the formula but her husband said she couldn't stay there, so off she went again with her baby. To Rosemary it felt as if her family and relatives all seemed to be telling her, *shame, shame on you..... a baby; unwed; no husband.* What had happened to this family? She thought are we doomed to disgrace and despair? Is that what occurs when you live to please only yourself?

34
rosemary's world

Rosemary had to move away to find work. Her Grand-parents were too old to be stressed out by having her and a newborn baby to care for and she rented a sleeping room. There was a woman there who agreed to keep the baby for her while she worked. After about a year of working nine hours a day, six days a week for twenty-one dollars, Rosemary had little to live on. She had rent and the baby-sitter to pay. There was very little money left for food, so she would eat at the restaurant where she worked.

While working Rosemary met a girl named Wanda. She was from Virginia and had come there to visit her parents. She asked Rosemary if she would like to go to Virginia with her and try to find work there. She said the pay would be better. Off she went with her son on the bus hoping for a better life. Rosemary found a nice lady to watch her son who was growing so fast. He was walking and beginning to talk and was a true delight. She found a job in a bar and was making good money. Life seemed good. The bar manager would always look for young girls to work for him. When she first arrived in Virginia with her son, the couple that owned the bar met Rosemary and her friend, Wanda. They had rented a sleeping room for the two women and paid for food for them to eat. They had also made arrangements for a lady to care for her son.

Rosemary started work by serving drinks to men who would come from the Navy ships on leave. The owner had hired ten or twelve girls to wear high-heels and pretty clothes and attract the sailors. They only talked to them and played pinball games. The girls never drank alcohol, just Kool-Aid that the sailors would buy them. She made good money and eventually she was able to rent a nice little apartment with a kitchen and a bathroom and even get some furniture. Life was better than it had ever been.

Rosemary still wrote her "fabrication" letters to her mother as she was too ashamed to tell her the truth. She really only wanted to be pleasing to her and to protect her from the real story… being still just a *bar* girl. She felt like she was the great pretender. Her Grandma would say there is no such thing as a white lie. Deep down she knew her Grandma was right. She felt so guilty inside. Rosemary knew her life was far from the one she would have wished for herself. *Dear God, it's so hard to make things right when they are so wrong.*

Then, out of the blue, when she least expected it, that's when she met a man and they began going out after work for something to eat. Rosemary thought he seemed to be okay with her already having a little boy. He was the only one she had ever dated. After about three months, he got out of the Navy and then went home to Nebraska. He promised Rosemary he would write to her. They talked on the phone and he told Rosemary that if she would marry him, he would come back to her. She made arrangements to go and see him and she was so happy.

They went to North Carolina to a Justice of the Peace and it was there that Rosemary was married. Unfortunately, he could find no work to support them. So Rosemary had to go to work to support them. Then she became pregnant again.

He watched her son and she worked until she was ready to give birth. This pregnancy was different from the first, she had only two sharp pains and suddenly began to hemorrhage. The police came and took Rosemary to the hospital where she gave birth, once again, she was all alone. However, she thought, at least this time she was married. Rosemary had given birth to a little girl. She was just beautiful and they named her Kimberlee Jo. But it was back to work for Rosemary. They lived in an upstairs apartment with no washer and dryer. She had to go to the Laundromat to wash and dry their clothes.

She didn't want her Mother to worry about her so she wrote her a letter. She told her some lies to make her think her life was good. She'd write things like she had married a widower from church with a good job.

How could I be so dumb to think that was a good idea?

Rosemary kept working in the bar and became pregnant again three months after her little girl was born. While she worked, her husband drank beer and complained that he still couldn't find work. When it was time for her to go to the hospital for the third time, once again she went there all-alone, as her husband had to care for the other two children. All night she labored and finally had a beautiful, big, healthy, baby boy. We named him Joseph Jeffery.

Little Joseph Jeffery was an arm full. When it was time for Rosemary to leave the hospital, she could barely carry him and her suitcase onto the bus.

When she got home with the baby, her husband was trying to be nice and he had made a pot of chili. They barely had enough money to buy the hamburger for the recipe. When he reached up above the stove to get the chili powder, he mistakenly picked up the pumpkin pie spice and poured some into the pot of chili. They had to eat it anyway because there was no other food in the house. When they looked at the bowl, it certainly looked like chili, but it tasted like pumpkin pie! Rosemary recalls what a laugh they had about this.

Within two weeks of giving birth, Rosemary went back to work. Her little boy was not quite four, her little girl was thirteen months and the new baby was just five weeks old. They had a hard time keeping our electric on or the heat on in the apartment. In the Virginia home, there was no heat in the bedrooms. She would put the new baby in the bassinet near the kitchen to keep him warm. On one cold night, she was awakened during the night by the crying of my three-year old son. She ran to comfort him and to her horror, she saw the new baby was hanging from the top rail of their little girl's crib. There was no sound. Rosemary screamed for her husband, he tried desperately to revive him but to no avail, it was hopeless. Rosemary ran outside, screaming for help. The police and firemen arrived but it was futile. Before too long a man came in carrying a big black suitcase, he took her precious baby boy away in the suitcase. What shock; what pain; what grief came into her life as a result of this tragedy. Rosemary went through the days like a zombie. The funeral was so sad and she wanted so badly to hold her baby boy, but she had to let him go. She held her other two little ones close.

The authorities wanted to place Rosemary's little son in a foster home for two years but she just couldn't allow that to happen. So her aunt and uncle took him into their home. It was the best mother and father she could give him at the time, as she was very sick with grief. She had to protect him from being placed in foster care.

Rosemary's empty arms ached as she continued to work in the bar as her husband still could not find work. Then when she was in such a bad time of her life, she became pregnant again. *I wonder why people do that. Her life is so unsettled and yet brings another child into the world.* Rosemary thought how easy it was for other people to judge her; she guessed that in her subconscious she wanted her baby back. She continued to work throughout her pregnancy, but they made her quit work two weeks before the baby was due to be born.

They were broke; they had no money to live on then with Rosemary not working. She would carry pop bottles back to the grocery store to get food money. It was finally time to go to the hospital to give birth for the fourth time, alone. Her husband had to stay with their little girl, so nothing had changed. Rosemary returned home from the hospital with their new baby boy who was nice and healthy.

Rosemary's lived a very poor life then. They had the electricity turned off several times and had to shower in the dark because they couldn't pay their bills. There were roaches running all over whenever the lights were turned back on. They were so dirt poor and Rosemary went back to work at a bar again and they finally were able to put food on the table again. One evening, while at work, Rosemary found a Bible in the ladies room. She turned the pages and it fell open to a Psalms passage that read, "I lay down and sleep even though ten thousand enemies come against me, and God sustains me."

That Psalm touched her heart so much and she wished, all of a sudden, that she could go to church. It was the first time she had even thought about God in a very long time. She thought what a bad girl I am, working in a bar.

Then one day she had a call from a woman she used

to work with in another bar. Her name was Joyce and she said if Rosemary could send her husband to Detroit, they would find work for him up there. So she scraped the money together and sent him on an airplane to Detroit, and he finally found work in Detroit. They found an apartment to live in and for the first time in a long while Rosemary didn't have to work.

She was happy to be able to stay at home with her children. She took them with her to church and it was then realized how good it would feel to go to a church. She went down to the front of the altar and gave my heart to God. She was baptized down into the water. She came up feeling clean and whole, she felt that Jesus really came into her heart that day. She was a new person changed from the inside out. Someone gave her a Bible and she began to read it for the first time.

They rented a house and got some furniture and the children had a yard to play in. Life would be good if only her husband would agree to go to church with them but that was not to be. He was on a roller coaster of sin with blind pigs and drinking continually.

Rosemary wrote her mother a few letters with pictures enclosed of the children. She just didn't want to get her hurt by John, whom she was married to. She was happy with God. Life was good. *Rosemary thought, why did it take me so long to realize that the way of the Bible is the right way to live. If I had not tried to run my own life, maybe I wouldn't have had to go through so much grief.*

Rosemary thought of her Grandma and Grandpa, who were both gone now. Grandpa died from a heart attack and one year later Grandma passed in her sleep. They both lived to be eighty years of age. Now they were laid side by side, in the cemetery next to the little Baptist church in Blooming Rose, West Virginia. What precious memories she has of them both. They had taken her into their home and their hearts. This was after raising so many of children of their own. "There was always room for one more" they used to say. Rosemary closed her eyes and could see her Grandpa reading his bible. He was a man of few words but with a big heart and Grandma was always singing as she worked. Oh, how she so enjoyed the small things in life like her flowers and the little children whenever she'd see them. Rosemary can still hear her voice ringing in her ears singing hymns. Rosemary knows she is in heaven with Grandpa. She silently hopes they know how much she has changed and how much she loved them both so dearly...and Jesus too.

35
becoming a nurse

The years seemed to pass quickly and Rosemary's children were growing up fast. Rosemary's little girl liked to learn her numbers and to read books. Her youngest son, Steve was four and liked to play with cars and trucks. Rosemary was content to cook and bake cookies. On the outside they appeared to look like a normal happy family.

The children and Rosemary went to church, but her husband stayed out late drinking beer a lot. Her heart ached for her baby who died. She often had nightmares of the night her baby died and would wake up crying. Her son Robert was with her aunt and doing well. She talked to her aunt about once a month on the phone. Though a large part of Rosemary's heart was breaking she knew life must go on.

Then came the day when Rosemary's husband came home and said "I just got laid off from work." He was so upset by that he couldn't even talk about it. *She wondered what would all this mean to us? We would have no income to pay our rent or utilities. What about food and health insurance?*

They had no money in the bank saved for a rainy day. Rosemary went down into the basement and started to pray ..."Please, God, you know our needs." She had read in the Bible about how God stilled the storm and saved the boat with his followers on board. *God, do you really care about my family, and me?* Rosemary thought. *Could you please still the storm in my life?* God must have heard her cries, for the very next day her husband was called back to work! All of their financial problems were solved but her husband still drank too much. God could not stop that, for he cannot make people not sin. Otherwise, we would be His puppets. Within a year Rosemary's husband bought them a home. It was a little, red, brick house with a porch and a fenced in backyard. Rosemary thought it was adorable. It had two bedrooms but they were able to put another bedroom in the basement because it had been finished off.

The Bible was a great joy for Rosemary as she learned many things about our Lord. Her children had a nice neighborhood to grow up in and their school was only two blocks away. Rosemary reflected on how her life was so much better than her poor Mother's had been. She thought about how, every day, we are faced with choices in our lives, some right and some wrong. If she had only made the right choices when she was sixteen years of age, maybe she would have followed a different path in her life.

Rosemary knew the very best decision she had made was when she had chosen God and to live a clean, decent life. If only she had only done this when she was sixteen, maybe she would have married a man who served God. She wished her sweet mother, Margaret, could have had a good life. If miracles could happen some way, maybe one day she could get out of her prison with that bad man, John. The other great wish Rosemary had was that somehow Grandma and Grandpa could look down from Heaven and know that she was doing better than just all right. She knew she was doing great because she had faith in God. He was her joy and knew how blessed she was to have her children in her life. They are growing up and they are a family. They all go to church together every Sunday. Her husband does well except he does refuse to attend church with them, however, he works and supports them and she is free to be a full-time mother to her children and not leave them to work.

Rosemary felt that, because she only went through the eighth grade, she wouldn't be able to go out and find a good enough job to support her family if something happened to her husband. She knew many men have heart attacks at a young age or they divorce their wife and leave them without any way of making an income. That possibility frightened Rosemary wand left her wondering what she would do if anything like that ever happened? She then decided then to do something about her situation. She went and got a book to study for a GED certificate. When she started to read the book, she became so overwhelmed that she put it aside. One day she was having a cup of coffee with a neighbor and mentioned the book on the GED test. She told Rosemary that she seemed intelligent enough and she urged her to take the test without the study guide. If she would miss on one section of the test, she could retake that part again. Rosemary had this on her mind and she told another woman who was also embarrassed about not having gone through high school. She said "Let's both go and if we don't pass we will not tell anyone."

The two women went in cold turkey and took the five part test and both passed and Rosemary even won a scholarship for two classes. She went straight to the community college to sign-up. She knew she wanted to be a Licensed Practical Nurse. They didn't have a course for the LPN but they did have a degree for an Registered Nurse. They said they didn't recommend that she take those classes because they were extremely difficult. Rosemary interrupted them and said, "Just give me the directions and I will begin."

She could not believe that she had passed the GED and in shock to think that she could go to college. Rosemary chose English and Speech classes and loved every day that she attended. Her husband made fun of her but she just kept going. After working hard for one year she had completed her liberal arts and was ready to apply for the nursing program. There were only two hundred and forty spots available and nine hundred applicants had applied. God came through again for her! Rosemary was accepted into the nursing program! On the first day of nursing school, she came home with her little white uniform on, excited and she was feeling good. It was then her husband informed her he was leaving her. She was shocked and deflated. *What could she do to change his mind?* He said that he needed to find himself. She told him that she would quit nursing school and give it all up if he would stay but he had made up his mind and he was leaving no matter what she did. While Rosemary was at school, he cleaned out his clothes closet and took the bedroom furniture with him. He wasn't really a good husband but he was the only one she had ever known. He just didn't seem to care for her or the children any longer. She almost died from the heartache. Just when she thought her life was going so well this had to happen.

Her life was a shambles once again. She had tried so hard to be a good wife and mother. The only thing she did was go to church with her children but she never preached to him or tried to force religion on him. She cooked him good meals and kept the house looking nice, as a good wife should. She was thirty-eight years old and she still looked pretty good. She kept her weight under control and tried to look her best when he was home. Then one day she heard from a friend that worked with him that he was living with a girl of twenty-one. His girlfriend was only four years older than their daughter, Kimberlee. Rosemary was shocked and hurt beyond belief. The ache in her heart was so painful that she could hardly breathe.

She knew that she had to survive and raise her children. Her daughter, Kimberlee was seventeen and so far a good girl. When her Father moved out, it rocked her world. Kimberlee then quit school and went to work in a diner.

Rosemary whispered in prayer, "Please, God, don't let her life go to pot like my Mother's and mine did." Rosemary cried and tried to keep going to school. Her son, Steve also quit school and was a troubled teen. She had her hands full now. Their father only gave a small amount of money to live on, however, they somehow managed to get by.

Rosemary later found out that the girl who had broken up their home, was pregnant with twins. Somehow she finished nursing school at forty years of age. It had to be God working in her life that allowed her to pass all the tests needed to become a Registered Nurse. Rosemary landed a job in a nice Catholic Hospital. From an eighth grade education to this, Rosemary knew it would take a miracle and God had performed one for her. That much she was sure of.

36
life with bill

Sometimes we can be up on a mountaintop, so high doing so well and survey the whole world. Be careful my friend, because you can slip and fall down and down you go so fast. Rosemary wished that, when she remarried, it would be a wonderful, Christian that provided a happily-ever-after life. Unfortunately, that was not to be for her. Women are weak at times when they find themselves alone danger lurking around every corner. She was not a bar girl anymore and she didn't drink alcohol or smoke. She was a hard worker, even working additional shifts in a nursing home to make extra money.

Her daughter, Kimberlee, had quit school because her life was turned upside down by her father leaving them. Rosemary went a little crazy herself at that time and was suffering with her own mid-life crisis. Kimberlee worked hard and passed the GED, just like Rosemary had. Then she married a man and had a wonderful daughter and then went to nursing school and became a registered nurse, just like her mother. Good things do happen in life.

Rosemary's son, Steve, also struggled but became a wonderful man and now lives on a fishing lake with his lovely wife. Rosemary now alone, finally came to her senses. She wrote many poems, mostly to God and she worked at her nursing job. However, she felt lost, and always alone and became depressed to the point of wanting to take her own life. She planned in her despair to jump in a very deep river and drown. However, God had different plans for her life.

Looking back, Rosemary thought, if she could have written a script and designed her own life it would go like this. She would love books and have a thirst for learning. She would continue in school and graduate high school. Then she would meet a young man who loved God with all his heart. He would ask her to church and have her catch the excitement of knowing Jesus along with him. He would ask her to be his wife, and they would spend their days and years of their lives in service to our God, our family and our country. They would have a wonderful child together that would be a product of their love. Life would be a fairy-tale, suited for the movies.

Rosemary thought, this is a foolish dream, but in reality, the day she met William, or Bill as she called him, was the very best next thing to happen to her. He picked Rosemary up from despair and she began a life that was finally stable. It took them both awhile to get straight because they were both broken and needed time to heal.

Bill grew up being a middle child. He had three siblings: an older brother, younger brother and one sister. His Dad worked very hard to provide a good living for the family and his mother stayed at home taking care of their family. She sometimes altered his Dad's suits over to fit the boys. Everyone in the family went to church except for his father. Bill was only four when he began kindergarten and lagged behind all his school years but still graduated. He delivered pizza and was a paper boy. He bought and paid for all his own clothes. He then went to work for Ford Motor Company. He married a pretty young woman and settled into a home. They had two wonderful children, a girl and then a boy. After sixteen years of being married his wife said she wanted to find herself and moved out and took the children with her and got a divorce. It left Bill alone and heartbroken.

It was then that Rosemary and Bill met. Rosemary too was lost and alone. They began spending time together and finally decided to get married. They lived in his home, now their home. Although their former spouses had abandoned them both they still valued the commitment and bonds of marriage.

As they took their wedding vows, Rosemary felt young and beautiful again. There were lots of people in the church, his parents, his sister and his two brothers attended. There was wedding cake and a dinner to celebrate their love. Rosemary's children were there and everyone was happy for them.

Together as One

Two shall become one? How can this be?
God was pleased to take a woman
and present her to a man.
His desire was for them to be one.
How really wonderful is life,
when two are joined together
with God as the head.
It's a perfect triangle of love
My prayer for you this day, with hands joined,
you would walk daily with your God
and look for ways to say
I Love You, a smile, a touch, and a quiet word.

Divide all your problems in two.
Take little faults and choose to forget it
in light of all the good you find in one another.
Draw close to you your God.
His love will flow down to bathe you and
your loved one all the days of your marriage.
May you be as one until death doth you part

Rosemary

Rosemary thought, *I wonder why it took me so long to find happiness and my real soul mate?* His name is William and she would sit and write it over and over. She was so happy to be his wife. She realized her ex-husband never did really love her. He only loved himself. She wished him well. He will have his hands full with a young wife and twins.

37
margaret breaks free

William and Rosemary traveled together and enjoyed stopping at the beaches in Florida and North Carolina. The first time she ever saw the big, blue, powerful ocean was with him. Life can be good when you try to do the right things in life. She only wished that she could have found him when she was a younger girl. She was forty-two when they met, but better late, than never. She did miss going to church at this time and often thought that maybe someday she and Bill would attend church together. For the first time in her life Rosemary finally had someone who really loved her and wanted to share his life with her. And when her children and grandchildren were also included in that love, Rosemary knew she had been blessed. She finally realized the happiness in her life she had always longed for.

Grandma would be amazed at the way she now lived She would be proud of her now that Rosemary has forgiven herself for all of her sins and bad choices in life. She wanted to just be a good person who served God. She only wanted to make choices that brought good things to her life.

At night when all is quiet, Rosemary allows herself to wander in her thoughts about life...

Roses are red and violets are blue.
Strange how you can cope when hopes and dreams don't come true.

She pushed it all down inside her subconscious mind when the pain was too hard to bear. At times during the night dreams or nightmares can occur. She would dream of how her little five week old baby son was taken away in death. She missed her son, Robert, who was lost to her in a different way. At least he is living in a good home with her aunt and uncle. Rosemary knew she was so blessed to have her daughter, Kimberlee and her son, Stephen. They were a joy beyond compare. We just need to go on in life taking the good with the bad. Some day we will all be united together in a better world. She tried to have faith and she wishes she could be more like the great woman her Grandma was. With all of her losses in her life, she still could smile and sing hymns. Grandma, would always be Rosemary's ideal, the one she most looks up to. Her Mother was great too, but she had so much pain in life to cope with.

Suddenly out of the blue, a crisis came in the form of a letter dropped in a mail box. Rosemary received a letter from her mother Margaret, informing her that she was coming to visit her in Michigan very soon.

She felt as though a fist had hit her in the stomach and the breath was knocked right out of her. The letter arrived early one morning enclosed in a long white envelope. She turned it over in her hands and read the return address. It was from her Mother. Rosemary's mouth grew dry and her hands began to tremble and become sweaty. Her Mother was writing to her and she was shocked. It had been such a long time without any contact between them. *What could this mean?* She wondered.

Rosemary's life was finally settled and she had a stable home now and a husband who took good care of her with two beautiful children. It had taken a long time to let go of her mistakes of the past. With the letter in her hands, the memories came rushing back to her. She had never known a father, nor brothers or sisters. The only life she had known was living with grandparents and sleeping in a small bed with her mother. She stuffed her mother's letter into her pocket. She was afraid to read how her mother always had a deep pain in her heart because she would love to be with Rosemary, her daughter, but she is stuck there with John and there is no way out. He has her in his trap .

Her Mother would write that she had a good feeling about God and she was reading her Bible and prayer helped her keep her sanity. She had found some joy in the planting of a few flowers in a wooden box on a little porch in the backyard and enjoying their leaves and the colors of each flower as they would bloom. She would gaze at the stars and the moon at night and enjoy them as well. Nature always reminded her that there was a Creator and it never failed to bring her hope.

Rosemary's life had changed and she finally had peace and was able to put the past behind her. Now, suddenly, she finds this letter in her mailbox from her mother. She was afraid to open it and put it in the pocket of her dress to wait until she could be alone to read the letter. Soon, the children will be in school and her husband will be at work.

She whispered a silent prayer to God and tore open the envelope. Reading the words brought tears to her eyes. *Dear Sweet Rosemary*...Her heart is touched by those words. Her mother, she knows, really does love her. She understands she has pushed many feelings for her down inside but now they come rushing to the surface. It takes a few moments before Rosemary can compose herself and continue to read that she is coming to see her. She has gotten away from John and was coming here in a few days! Rosemary was happy but also frightened. She wanted desperately to see her mother but she didn't want anything to upset this life she had now built. She was anxious to tell my husband and children, though so many questions continued to run inside her head. *Will she need to live with us? What about the children? Maybe it would be nice for them to have a Grandmother around? I wonder what she looks like now? Does she still drink?* It was amazing how one little letter could suddenly unleash feelings that had been long buried deep inside her heart.

Rosemary continued reading and had discovered her mother had found God and was a changed person. It would be like meeting a perfect stranger. Rosemary thought, *God help me to have compassion and to forgive her for her past.* Perhaps they could have a relationship…after all, she *is* my mother. She began to cry when she realized that her Mother was free. No more beatings or fearfulness.

When Rosemary told her family about the letter she had received from her Mother they were amazed, but happy. "Grandma is coming?" "When," they asked. All of the children seemed to be really excited about her visit. Her husband was anxious to meet her as well but there was still a small, nagging reluctance on Rosemary's part after all these years to open her home and her heart.

When the day arrived, Rosemary gathered the children into the car and they drove to the Greyhound Bus station to meet her. She would be coming in at noon. They waited and watched for her bus. Rosemary couldn't believe her eyes when the door opened, her eyes darting back and forth and then finding her Mother on the top landing. Rosemary stood frozen at the bottom looking up at her and then her Mother whispered, "My daughter, my girl." Before Rosemary knew it, she was in her arms, and her Mother was sobbing!

What a joy...she was actually here and she was happy. The children seemed a little shy at first but then each one allowed her to hug them closely. Afterwards, they stood and watched their grandmother wrap her arms around Rosemary who welcomed her embrace. Surprisingly Margaret looked very well to Rosemary. She was not at all as old looking as Rosemary had feared she would. She knew that this would be a special time for everyone.

38
margaret's diary

Dear Diary,

How could this be? The Bible speaks of sin or a curse going through ten generations. I guess it meant me as I had no money and no way to help my own daughter.

I am trapped in my own kind of Hell just living with John. He had discovered a bad sin that I had committed when I was young and he held it over my head. No one else knew. I was in a trap. I walked the floor crying and praying to God for mercy, but He seemed so far away. Please help my daughter, Rosemary. I cannot go to her because John has threatened to reveal my dark secret if I do.

My cousin has promised that she is safe and in a Home for Unwed Mothers and her needs are being met. Anyway, she isn't ready to talk to me because she is so ashamed. Through letters and phone calls, my cousin keeps me informed.

One day, while shopping, I came across a red diary, which only cost seventy-five cents. I needed any kind of an outlet as I had no one to talk to about my feelings. I bought the diary and decided I would write in it each day. Perhaps, someday my daughter would be able to read my words and understand more fully the life I led and some of the reasons why we needed to live apart.

That very night, when John wasn't around, I sat in my chair with the diary in my lap, and wondered where to begin. After all, I thought, this is for Rosemary and it will be my story.

Dear Diary...I began

I wanted to write of the wonder of you. The first time that I held you, my heart overflowed with love for you.

How could it be that something so wonderful as you could come from me? As I touched your little face and looked deep into your eyes, the world seemed to stand still. My joy. I counted all of your perfect fingers and toes. The best feeling was when your rose bud mouth searched and found my breast. I'm broken hearted that I brought you into this world without a daddy. I promise to love and care for you to the best of my ability as long as I have a breath.

You will be my joy forever.

Dear Diary,

I so wanted to tell you, my daughter, of the tears I shed after sending you away, first to live with my parents and then again after your tragic occurrence. I had to once more send you away with my cousin to live in Cleveland. I was always sending you away. When all I ever wanted was to keep you with me. In the long run, a mother always tries to do what's best for her child. I truly understand what you feel and what you are going through. The time will pass and soon you will know the greatest joy God can give you. Your very own precious baby. When you hold that baby, all else will fade away and you will be happy once more.

You must remember that we all make mistakes. God knows I did. Hold your head high. There was a time I went through *all the same guilt and shame. If only you knew how much I wanted to be with you and help you through this time.*

Dear Diary,
I got your letter today. A grandson. How wonderful. Oh, how I wish I could see you, and put my arms around you and let you know how proud I am of you. I know you have been too ashamed to talk to me. If only you knew that if I could, I would have been there for you and understood and helped you.. If I wasn't in a prison of my own making. I think I aged five years. When I heard you were in a home for unwed mothers and then to have given birth all alone but now, I rejoice. Your baby is born a boy...flesh of my flesh. I have a grandson! I wish I could spend my days just being a good grandmother.

I would like to forget my past and start anew and just be a sweet granny but, that's not to be at this time. I began to save a little money and go to church, that is as often as John would allow it. I read God's word and have some hope that all is not lost. Has the Lord heard my prayers? Perhaps the curse is lifted as John is spending less time at home. His mind appears to be somewhere else and he seems happier. When he is happier there are fewer beatings and fear but even with this anger I don't try to leave. Things are the way he wants them and they had better stay that way. Today's mail brought me another letter from an old neighbor of mine.

Margaret had known Martha since they were young girls. The both lived up in the coal mining town of Burnwell, West Virginia. She had moved to the town of Hanford a few months after Margaret had met Wyatt Kindall. That's where he lived with his family. Martha wrote Margaret letters off and on telling her about his marriage. Margaret didn't respond to Martha's letters as she didn't like him or his wife and she was in a depression mode. Martha knew of the disgrace brought on to Margaret because of her pregnancy. Margaret did write back to her once, asking her not to write now that she lived with John. She would get a beating every time a letter came in her name. He accused Margaret of telling lies to make people feel sorry for her.

It is a fearful thing to have the door shut and be locked in, and then to see the anger in a man's face when he refuses to listen to reason. He only wants to hit and kick you while you are down. Many times she thought about her family. All of her brothers and sisters who were now grown up, as well as, the nieces and nephews who she'd never even seen. Her whole family is lost to her as John keeps her in his own trap. No one is allowed to contact her as he has changed their phone number. He watches the mail for any letters that Margaret might receive. Her mother came to see her one time and when she saw the bruises and the fear in Margaret's face, she said that it was better for Margaret if no one contacted her. Margaret watched her leave and felt such deep grief. She had learned that her father was ill, with many problems and too weak to come and visit her. Mother said that she would pray for her daily. Her first duty at that particular time was to tend to Margaret's father.

John threatened her and said she would be sorry if her family came to see her ever again. He said she belonged to him and to him alone. One day, a neighbor lady came to see Margaret after John was gone in the morning.

39
the grandchildren

Margaret's joy knew no bounds, as another letter came in the mail. Pictures fell out. They were of her grandchildren, a little boy named Robert and a little girl named Kimberlee. There was another picture of Rosemary, standing outside her house. Yes, she has a house, a home of her own. The wonder of it all. She looked happy as she smiled in the picture. My sweet girl is going to be alright after all. How Margaret would like to be a part of her life and be near her and the children.

She writes to Rosemary, She's different now and has lost her desire for drinking. She doesn't want any part of that kind of life anymore. She so wishes that she had a second chance to start all over again. She is sending some money for birthday gifts for the children and secretly hopes she doesn't get caught. Now and then she is able to hide a little from her house money. John would be so angry with her and would probably kill her if he knew. Not that her life really matters anymore. She just wants to bless her family with a small gift now and then.

She decides she will send it out today when the mailman comes by.

She went to the mailbox and found a letter from her daughter and rushed inside to open it. She was so glad John was out for the day. She wanted to be alone to read her daughter's sweet words. Margaret's heart ached from missing her so much. Rosemary has been in Cleveland with her nephew. The last she had heard she was working in a five and dime store.

Mother,

How are you? I hope all is well with you and that John is being nice to you." I wish that some day ,we could live near one another, and share our lives together.

I love you, very much. All is going good with me.

Your daughter;
Rosemary

The night closed in and the time passed quickly. She was lost in her own world.

Engrossed in her thoughts, she fell asleep in her over -stuffed chair with her Bible on her lap. She didn't even hear John when he came home. The door slammed ,and she was suddenly awakened by his stumbling into the room.

"I'm hungry. Why are you sleeping?" John demanded.

She could smell the foul liquor on his breath. His eyes were red and blood shot and he looked like he had slept in his clothes. They were wrinkled and soiled. He didn't come home last night but stayed out with friends, or at least that's what she thought.

Fear gripped her and she began to move away. "Rest here", she told John as she pointed to a chair, and I'll fix you some food." She was moving toward the kitchen the whole time she spoke. She wanted to quiet him down, hoping to avoid a scene. "There is never any food to eat in this house. All you ever do is read that Bible." John stated. He grabbed it from her hand and tossed it across the room. "Don't be mad, I will fix you something nice to eat and you can rest here awhile." Margaret rushed to the kitchen and started to heat some food in a pan. Chicken always seemed to please him and she was glad she had cooked some earlier. Her hands shook as she put some biscuits in the oven to warm. She was so thankful to hear him snoring. He had fallen asleep in the chair. He looked so lost. She wished she could help him but that is not possible with someone who refuses to listen.

Their life was so unsettled and so prone to someone being hurt. Someday she is afraid he will kill her or injure her beyond any help. She wishes she could get away before it's too late. *Where could I go? How could I live on my own?* Someday maybe God will make a way for this to take place as miracles still happen.

40
the great escape

One day, coming into the house, John fell down drunk
as usual. He hit his head on the front step and blood was
running down his face. Margaret called a neighbor to help
her get him up but John wouldn't wake up. Their life was
so unsettled, so prone to hurt. Margaret lives in fear that
someday he will kill her or injure her beyond recognition.
She wished she could get away, but how would she ever
live on her own? Someday, perhaps God will make a way
for this to happen. Margaret believed that miracles still
can happen.

They arrived at the hospital and after what seemed an
eternity, the doctor came out and talked to her. He told
her that John would be okay. He had a slight concussion
and needed to be watched for a few days. Because there
was a head injury involved, he recommended that John
stay a few days in the hospital. *A few days in the hospital? Margaret's mind was already working. Maybe this could
be the chance she had been hoping for. A plan...that's what she
needed. . . a plan. She could get away and it would be days*

before he even knew it. Money! She needed money. She only had a small amount squirreled away but it was not enough for a new start. The government check would be coming…that was her answer.

The mailman put the check in the mailbox. Margaret knew instantly what it was. Her hands grew sweaty as she opened the envelope. She had practiced signing John's name for a long time. She didn't know why she did that, but as she signed his name to the check sure she knew no one would be able to tell that it wasn't his signature. Margaret's heart was beating so fast that it felt like a trip hammer in her chest. She couldn't believe it was actually happening. Now, just maybe she could really get away.

She thought that anyone standing near her could hear her heart beating hard. She took a deep breath and whispered, "Please God, I know this is wrong but it may be my only chance. Please help me get this check cashed."

The teller smiled at her and asked where John was. Margaret said, "He is in the hospital." She counted out the money and handed it to her saying, "I hope John is better soon."

She couldn't believe it had actually worked. Maybe she really could get away from John. Now, *where do I go?* She remembered Rosemary's offer to live with her. It had been out of the question before but now that she had cashed the check she had to leave before John found out what she had done.

She only had a few things to pack and only a few things actually meant anything to her. She practically ran all the way to the bus terminal, continually looking around and behind her, half expecting to see John at any moment. With the money now in her purse, she was on her way. She saw a postal box at the corner and reached in her pocket for the note she had written to Rosemary saying she would be coming for a visit. She slipped the note into the post box and knew that from that point there would be no turning back.

There were three people ahead of Margaret in line waiting to buy tickets. She was frantic and in a constant state of fear. It was finally her turn. She purchased her ticket and watched the clock for the time of departure. She heard the bus was boarding and finally began to feel a little more at ease. She was on her way to Detroit. She fell into the seat and wondered if the people around her could hear her heart pounding.

Then after what seemed like hours, the door closed and the bus began to move. She had made it! She was finally going to be free! Margaret thought that nothing could happen to her in the future could be as bad as the past ten years with John. He had mental problems and they made him a Jekyll and Hyde. She hoped that she would never see him in this life again. Margaret sat back in her seat. No one sat next leaving her alone with her thoughts.

Here she was running away again! However, this time, it would be different. She hadn't had a drink in years. She was through with the seedy side of life. She wanted only peace, a job and a way to earn her own way. At least, she had enough money to tide her over until she could find a job.

41
the bus ride

When she first got on the bus, Margaret's hands were shaking. Now her heart began to beat normally although her mind was still racing. As the distance between John and Margaret grew, she began to relax. She had different anxieties and concerns now, but at least the physical pain was over. Suddenly she had a flashback. It was just after a night of rage and abuse. John had passed out and she had just finished cleaning up her injuries. Looking at herself in the mirror and wondered how much more of this she could take. She looked around the bedroom and noticed his jacket was lying on the floor. She picked it up to put it in the closet and felt something heavy inside the pocket. She laid the jacket on the bed and reached in the pocket with fear gripping Margaret's entire body.

She just knew instinctively, by the feel of it, that it was a gun. *Was it meant for me?* She realized for the very first time that he was capable of killing her. Should she wait for that fateful day to happen or should she do it herself? After all, she felt worthless and thought what difference would it make anyway. She felt the cold metal of the gun and placed it inside her mouth. As her lips closed around the barrel, she caught an image of Rosemary smiling at her. She looked so pretty, the last time she saw her. Margaret didn't want to live, but she didn't want to cause the people she loved any more pain. So she removed the gun from her mouth and started thinking of places to hide the gun. What if John woke up and caught her? Quickly, she placed the gun in the bottom drawer of her dresser. then got down on her knees and cried, "God forgive me!"

She vowed then to live until it was her time to die unless John kills her first, which she now knew was a daily possibility. Now, on the bus and racing away from John's brutality her thoughts returned to the present and her chance at a new life. She was thankful that she hadn't ended her life that day. She was also thankful for her daughter's life. With closed eyes her thoughts went forward to seeing Rosemary and her grandchildren.

Now you have the story of how Margaret was finally able to escape the abuse and horror of John. We turn the pages as she begins her new life.

Our choices affect not one but many other people in our lives. Life is like a pebble tossed upon the water and the rings spread far and wide. Pause now and take a look at Rosemary's saga.

Margaret has been forcibly shut off from the world by John. She has had from time to time letters from her family and a few from her daughter. She has heard many conflicting stories about her. She was unsure of the real truth. The only thing that she really cared about was to finally be able to see her sweet girl and grandchildren. Whatever else happened she would cope with it. Any life would have to be better than the way she had lived in the past. She thought, if I could just be with my daughter again, then I would be happy to pass on. My dreams would have come true.

Margaret took out her ink pen and an old lined tablet she had hidden in the travel bag and wrote a poem about her daughter. She had written poems many times in the past but had never let anyone else see them. But this time she would, God willing, if she made it to Detroit. Margaret vowed she would personally give it to her lovely daughter...

She folded the pages and said to herself, *Yes, I think she will like this little poem from me.* She put it away inside her purse and closed her eyes in rest. The movement of the bus had a cadence as she traveled along mile after mile. The bus was only about half full, so Margaret had both seats to herself. Looking around she noticed so many people of different ages and color of skin. All were going up north and each had a story to tell. They each were in their own little world avoiding eye contact with each other. Occasionally, someone would look over at her and probably wonder about her. She was like a scared rabbit but she was finally free. As the darkness of night closesd in, she found herself looking through the window. The moon hung bright and a beautiful orange glow gave it the appearance of a huge pumpkin in the sky.

Almost everyone else on the bus was asleep or lost in their own thoughts. Margaret wondered about John. She has always been fearful of him and, at times, hated the very sight or sound of him. Deep down she felt sorry for him. What a monster he had been. Yet, a glimmer of kindness once in a while would appear. She knew he was a sick man in many ways. Margaret hoped he would get the help he so desperately needed.

The only thing she knew now was that she hoped to never have to lay eyes upon him again as long as she lived. She thought, *I know I'm weak or I would have tried to get away sooner. But better late than never. I am on my way now, Praise God! No matter what my future holds, I will be happy. I could eat bread and water and live in a shack. Nothing matters but my freedom and having quietness and peace.*

42
a new beginning

On arriving in Detroit and seeing her family, Margaret was overcome with the emotion of the moment. She didn't know how long they held each other. She had waited for so long for this day to arrive and now the day was finally here.

Rosemary invited her to stay with them, but as much as she wanted to, she didn't want to be an inconvenience. They talked it over and Rosemary agreed to help her find a room. She said she knew of a nice lady about two miles from her that rented rooms. She took me there to look at the rooms. It was more than she needed but she was so happy to have a place so close to her family. Mostly, she was grateful to finally have a key of her own. Imagine? A key to her own room. It had been so long since she could lock her door and lock out the world if she chose to do so. They said their goodbyes, with plans for them to pick her up the next day and go to their home for dinner. Margaret couldn't wait for tomorrow but when the door closed behind them, she looked around and couldn't believe her eyes. The room had immaculate order and quietness surrounded her. She was safe with no more crazy days and nights and no more walking the floor in fear.

That evening she got a visit from her new landlady, Mrs. Turner. It was so nice to have a visitor. It had been a long time since she was allowed to have a friend of her own. Margaret told her briefly about her coming to live in Michigan to be near her family and that she would be looking for work in the area. Mrs. Turner mentioned that the Kresgge dime store was hiring and it was within walking distance of her home. Margaret was excited and encouraged but first she would spend a day with her family.

The next morning, after her first restful night's sleep in a very long time, she arose early and decided to take a walk. Mrs. Turner heard her stirring and knocked on her door to invite Margaret for tea and toast. She told her how to get to Kresgee's and Margaret was anxious to know if they might hire her, after all she was a woman in her fifties with no references. It was a beautiful day September day. The leaves had begun to turn gold and orange. She'd seen this all before, but never like this. Everything was a new experience. A whole new world was opening up before her eyes.

The first street was lined with old Victorian homes but as she came closer to the main street, she could see small stores, a gas station and Kresgee's Five and Dime. Before she arrived, she caught a glimpse of herself in a store-front window. *I hope my skirt isn't too long.* She tucked her blouse in neatly around her waist and ran her fingers through her short brown hair.

She never had any other kind of job except for wait-ressing and for that she wore a uniform. *I hope I'm not too much out of style. I wish I had some decent clothes. Oh well, too late to worry about that now.* She stood tall, gathered all the courage she could muster and headed for the door. The interview was brief and before she knew it she had a job. She couldn't believe it, she was hired, it had been ten years but, at last, she had a job. Now she was very excited. *I should pick up a few things for my family*, she thought.

43

reconnecting

On the walk back to the house, Margaret felt light on her feet. It was as though the weight of the world had been lifted from her shoulders. She didn't need much...a room to sleep in and a little food. Her daughter had said she was glad that she was coming to see her. John didn't know her address. Michigan was a big place. In twenty-four hours her life had finally changed. She slept on and off but still felt nervous and fearful. *What if this didn't work out?*

It was noon before she knew it and Rosemary was at her door. She looked at herself in the mirror and hoped that she was what her daughter expected.

When they got into the car Rosemary smiled at Margaret, she turned on the engine and took her hand in hers. She tried to describe her husband to Margaret. "He's five years older than me, has reddish hair and a beard." she giggled. She knew she would instantly love this man. After all, he had been good to her daughter and they had built a life together and she certainly seemed happy.

Margaret hoped he didn't think too badly of her now that she really had changed her life. She hoped that he being a man of God would have compassion. Rosemary told her not to worry because Bill was a kind man. There was a moment of silence and then Rosemary said, "I was so surprised to get that letter from you. I must tell you, my prayers have been answered. I have wanted you to leave that man forever."

Rosemary confessed that there were times in her life, that she had love-hate feelings toward her. Now she said, she realized it was wrong to judge her. No one could really know what another person's life was like except that person. You made decisions based on what was happening in your life at that time. "You are my mother, and now that I have children of my own, I have a little more understanding of your choices."

Rosemary told her that she was just so overwhelmed when she thought of her mother living with John for so long. "When you said that you were coming, I had mixed feelings." Rosemary admitted that she was a little fearful. She had also been bad too. *Who was she to judge her Mother?* Now she was so lucky to be happy in her life.

Rosemary confessed that when she saw her getting off that bus, her heart skipped a beat and she knew then it would be all right. She just wanted to say to Margaret, "welcome to my life, dear mother".

Rosemary said, "Now, let's hurry home as the others are anxiously waiting to get to know you. The children were a little shy yesterday when they saw you. In time they will grow to love you as I do."

Margaret was silent as her daughter poured out her heart to her. She just wiped away the tears from her eyes and held on to her daughter's hand. No matter what she could say to me, she knew she would always love this sweet girl. It was good for her to clear the air though so they could begin anew.

Margaret was so happy, *Glory Hallelujah*, she thought, *I am free! It's like a new birth.* First, she saw her daughter was truly happy; she has wonderful children, a nice home and a good husband. *God truly has answered my prayers* she thought. She would live a life of joy with no more John and no longer the fear of being beaten. She has a little peaceful place to live. She gets to go to church. She sings, and most of all she prays that she will be forgiven.

The people at church didn't know of her past. They accepted her as a Christian mother and grandmother.

They drove down a small tree lined street. Most of the trees seemed to be live oaks. The houses were all alike. Only the colors on the outside made them different. Yards were neat and flowers grew all around. The garden of Eden couldn't be any prettier she thought.

Rosemary's house was blue with white trim with a white rocker was on the porch. As they pulled into the driveway, the front door flew open and out ran two of the most precious children. Her joy knew no bounds. Then, a very tall man came out of the house with a shaggy little dog whose name she discovered was Mocha. The man walked up to her and said, "Welcome, Margaret." His smile was so sweet. She thought he had the kindest eyes she had ever seen.

His name was Bill. God had blessed her daughter with this wonderful man and family. What more could a mother ask for? At first, her grandchildren were a little shy to meet her but when she gave each one a little gift, they seemed to forget that she was a stranger. Soon after they watched their mother and grandmother hug, which brought smiles to everyone and a room filled with joy. The ice was broken and both of the children allowed Margaret to hug them also.

The afternoon passed too quickly for them. It was

pleasant catching up on so many occasions in their lives. They looked at picture albums and it gave Margaret a glimpse of their past. The children giggled as they looked at their baby pictures with their bare butts and their eyes lit up when they saw photos of themselves dressed in their Sunday best. As the children turned the last page in the album, Kimberlee looked up with curiosity. "Grandma — do you have any pictures of when you were a little girl?" "No dear, we were too poor to have pictures taken when I was growing up", Margaret explained. After a wonderful home-cooked meal, it was time for Margaret to be on her way. Rosemary promised the children they would see their Grandma again soon. She asked Margaret if she wanted to go to church with them on Sunday. Margaret beamed with happiness and smiled, answering with a simple, "yes."

She could hardly wait for Sunday to arrive. No one here knew of her past and she would truly start out brand new. So many times in the past she had wished she could have lived a different life; one of obedience, one that was pure. Now, she realized that only wishing things had been different was truly a waste of time. She needed to let the past go and enjoy the opportunity that God had given her.

She even began teaching a Bible study class for little six year old children which brought her joy. They turn their sweet faces up to her and listen as she teaches the stories of our Lord. She wonders at how can it be that one such as her could be so blessed?

44

good news...bad news

The days and weeks seemed to fly by. Margaret enjoyed her work and found herself smiling and even walking with a skip. It was hard to believe that her life could be so good. She finally felt at peace and rarely thought of John now. However, when she did, she realized she didn't have to be afraid anymore. She knew he would survive because the bad ones always do. Margaret started to gain a little weight and her hair looked better with a shorter style. She even bought a few new pieces of clothing.

Margaret was also getting to spend quality time with her daughter and she helped her to pick out some clothes. She didn't know much about style and she sure needed Rosemary's help.

Margaret also worked at a soup kitchen run by her church on Saturdays, handing out food to the needy. How well she could understand the pain she saw in the faces of these people. How she wanted to tell them that Jesus is the answer. She passed out a tract booklet to anyone who will accept it. It explains God's plan of salvation. Her favorite Bible verse is John 3:16...God so loved the world that He gave His only Son that whosoever shall believe in Him shall not perish but have everlasting life.

She read her Bible daily and even joined a Bible study group. It really brought joy to her life and to her pleasant surprise, everyone at church seemed to accept her. At times she felt like such a hypocrite. No one knew of her sinful past but she felt that God had forgiven her. She was ready to live a good clean life. After weeks of preparation, the day had finally arrived for Margaret to be baptized. She wore a white robe and, as she stepped into the water as a sinner, she knew she would be cleansed of all her sins. The preacher took her by the hand. He said the words, "I baptize thee in the name of the Father, Son and the Holy Spirit." He then eased her under the water. She was completely submerged. As the water covered her, she felt the burden of sin released. When she came up out of the water, she was a new person. Her family had witnessed her rebirth and rejoiced with her. Margaret thought, *How could it be that a God so great could love me? How could it be that life could be so good?* A smile seemed to be continually on her face. Now she lives in peace with want of nothing. She loves her work and her little apartment is so quiet and peaceful. She is truly a happy and contented woman.

Margaret's son-in-law seemed to enjoy her company. She was invited to have holidays with the family. How wonderful it was for her to share meals and feel the love from so many. The years seemed to pass ever so swiftly and Margaret's affection grew for her son-in-law. Her heart swelled with joy as they attended church together and a quiet dinner at their home. Later, when she would close the door of her little apartment, she would feel wonderfully blessed, beyond measure, by God. She felt such gratitude for her life. God had truly performed a miracle in her life. As bad as she had been, He had turned her from an ugly caterpillar into a beautiful butterfly. Margaret went to Bible study and made new friends at work and church. At times she felt like a hypocrite but she could never allow any one of them to know about her awful past. For the first time in her life she felt like a whole person. She shuttered to think of all the years she wasted in sin and by the wrong choices she kept on making.

Margaret's life of sin had taken its toll on her health. She had severe pain from the broken back but she tolerated the physical pain, which to her was bearable. It was the emotional pain that wore her down. This was Margaret's story, as she laid out her life. Wouldn't it be nice if it could end this way, but, alas, that was not to be.

Margaret went to the doctor with a chronic cough. She hadn't wanted to see a doctor because she didn't want to tell anyone about her drinking of years past. She had tried to bury that, but as it of ten does fate has a way of rearing its ugly head. After many tests, she realized she had waited too long. The doctor broke the news to her that she had developed lung cancer and it was progressing rapidly. He couldn't say how long she would have to live but the doctor looked grim as he explained her condition to her. She would need to wear constantly carry oxygen with her to breathe and her cough was her constant companion now. She was also unable to continue working any longer. She felt only sadness for her daughter Rosemary and her family.

45
the picnic

The news of Margaret's condition was bad and she hurt for her daughter. She had caused her so much pain in her life, when all she ever really wanted was to bring joy to her family. She tried to spread love in every way that she knew how since coming to live near her. Little gifts were given and she spent time playing games and making funny faces at the children. She could never make up for the wasted years, but there was so much pleasure in just loving them all now while she could.

There was so much love overflowing from her heart to them. She felt their soft skin and hugged them back as she tucked the little ones into bed.

Most of all seeing the family at church gave her such a peaceful feeling. She could see that God was continuing to bless this family.

When Margaret looked at herself in the mirror, she was amazed to see a round little snow haired lady looking back at her. One who wore a constant smile on her face? Making her many wrinkles disappear with a smile. She thought, *I truly have become a Granny.* Yes, it seemsedthat this was her new name because most everyone called her by that now. People at church, in her Bible study class, neighbors and of course her grandchildren, even her daughter called her Granny. Margaret thought, *these days are the best,* serving Jesus in any way she can. It makes up for her suffering in years past. Since she moved to Detroit, she had often wanted to say so many things to her daughter but seemed to not find the right words.

The diary she had begun to write in many years ago had allowed Margaret to pour out so many feelings to Rosemary. She hopes to leave this little book for her to read after she's gone perhaps.

It will allow her the opportunity to look deeply into her heart where there is painted a portrait of a life lived in the wrong way, with many of the wrong choices. She wants her also to realize what a good and wonderful God we serve. Throughout the years that Margaret had been writing here in her journal, she had wept many times over the words, fearful that the tears would blur the ink and she wouldn't be able to read the message.

One morning as Margaret was relaxing in her arm chair watching television, she heard voices and a gentle knock on the door.

She wasn't feeling very well but she heard the giggling of the children outside her door. *What a surprise!* Her daughter Rosemary and the children were standing there with all smiles and a picnic basket filled with food. They came to spend the day with her as she had become too weak to get out anymore. "Granny," they squealed, "we're going to have a picnic right here on your little table!"

Rosemary spread out a tablecloth and the children scurried to fill the table with their goodies. Margaret sank back down into her chair and was overjoyed just watching her family preparing their picnic for her. Margaret would have needed oxygen, if they had gone outdoors, but she didn't want to frighten the children by the sight of it. She had to move slowly to conserve her breath. She may have been weak, but she was still very happy. She called for Kimberlee and brushed her soft blond hair and put in a pink ribbon. She whispered in little Steve's ear... "Look in Granny's top drawer, there's a little surprise in there for you." There was a small bracelet for Kim and marbles for Steve. She always tried to keep little surprises for them.

His eyes lit up when he picked up the marbles and he handed the bracelet to Kim. They ran to their Granny and hugged her, thanking her over and over. It was a wonderful day and that night Margaret had pleasant dreams.

46
margaret's death

The next morning when Margaret awoke, she was gasping for a breath. She called Rosemary and she said she would pick her up to take her to the doctor's office. She was grateful to have her oxygen to help her to try to get her breath. The ride seemed longer than usual.

There were other patients in the waiting room when they arrived but the receptionist sent them right in. After examining her, the doctor made the suggestion that she sleep on a recliner to help ease her breathing. Margaret sensed he was not telling her the whole story. She asked Rosemary to bring the car around, and after she was out of ear shot, she asked the doctor to tell her exactly where she stood. She told him that she could handle hearing this news.

The doctor said it would be a matter of weeks, not months before the end. He said she could go to the hospital from there or she could stay at home for as long as she wanted if she didn't panic. Margaret thanked him for his honesty and said it would be her choice to go to the hospital. She asked the doctor if she could have one more day at home before going to the hospital. He smiled and said, "Of course you can."

She was sorry she had to tell her daughter this news. "Don't cry my sweet one." She said, as she held her close, "It will be alright".

Margaret said, "Please, let's go and get the children and play one more time at the park. Then we'll stop for some ice cream and tonight I want to read them their bedtime story and tuck them in just one more time. They are the joy of my life. We have so many blessings to be thankful for."

Rosemary smiled through her tears. "The children love you so Mom; and you know I really do love you too. You never cease to amaze me with your faith. I will try and be brave for the sake of the children."

Margaret took her hand in hers and for the first time she told her of the diary that she had been using to express some of her heart-felt feelings. She requested that after she was gone, that Rosemary go off alone to a quiet place of solitude and read it. Her hope was that this would tell her the true story of her mother's love. When you finish it, she said, there is still one more thing to be revealed to you, which is for your eyes only.

Rosemary read, *You have said you often wondered why I stayed with John through all the abuse. I have to confess, that John found out about my secret and held it over my head all those years. It is the main reason I stayed with John as long as I did.*

Rosemary continued reading, *One night while having a nightmare, he found out my sin of the past. When finally, what seemed to be my last chance, I took the opportunity to get out when John went into the hospital. It was then I left. I need to clear my conscience before I face my God and Maker. I pray God can forgive me.*

When they arrived at the hospital and after what seemed to be endless paperwork, Margaret was assigned to a room. Rosemary went with her and after receiving medication and a breathing treatment, she was reasonably comfortable.

The medication began to kick in. Margaret was in the process of telling her how much she appreciated Rosemary allowing her back into her life. She summoned her to come closer, as sleep was overcoming her. She told her, "You have been a joy to me from your very first cry to the hug you gave me when I got off the Greyhound bus. Even when we weren't together, you were always in my thoughts. Please don't be sad. I am not afraid to die. I am almost looking forward to ridding myself of this old body which isn't good for much anymore anyway. I am looking forward to seeing my parents and thanking them once more for their love and support.

She said, dear daughter, in heaven you really do have a Father and there is no shame there. We will truly be a family. I had the most wonderful dream. I had entered the kingdom of Heaven and left this body behind. I was free. I felt like a butterfly that had just burst forth from the cocoon. Her words began to become further and further apart as the medication began to work. She felt her daughter's lips touch her cheek and her hand brush across her forehead. She pushed the hair from her face and she heard her whisper,

"I love you Mama. Sleep well and I'll see you in the morning."

Margaret lay quietly in the hospital bed. Only the sound of the oxygen machine was heard. She was breathing better now as the medicine opened her lungs. She watches as Rosemary leaves the room to go home to her family. She says, "Goodnight my sweet girl ."

Margaret recalls that all of her life Rosemary has been

such a blessing to her. They had forced separations at different times that Margaret thought were mostly her own fault. Still, she had always loved and admired her daughter. She loved the way she walked, the sound of her laughter. She brought me such joy.

Throughout the day she found her body was growing weaker but her faith seemed to be growing stronger. God is my constant companion, she thought. As she read His word and prayed, she really doesn't fear death. She only wished she could of lived longer with her family and watched her grandchildren grow up to be adults. This, however, was not to be. God had other plans for her. At times a feeling comes over her, it's almost like homesickness, she has a longing to go and be with the Lord. She is grateful for so many things. Most of all it's that no one could ever imagine that she was ever a bad woman of the streets.

Margaret ponders how her life has evolved from a nice girl growing up to a little round shaped old Granny. This brings her such an inner joy. Thank you God, she prays you have truly blessed me. She wonders how she can tell Him of the love that's in her heart today. Her heart is overflowing with gratitude. She at that wrote a love letter to her God. Then, anyone who reads this will know that she truly loved Jesus. On pretty paper with a border of purple flowers she had penned these words...

Oh wondrous God, at times I lose the words to tell you of my great love for you. Some glad day by your grace and mercy, I will sing around your throne. In Heaven I will forever tell of your love to save a sinner such as me. Yes, I will bless your name. What love, where in you loved us, to send forth Jesus to take our place on the cross? Jesus understood that love; when a bad woman was caught committing adultery. He said, "Where are your accusers?" Looking around, He said He who is with-

out sin cast the first stone."
He had great compassion for sinners such as me. His
precious blood was given to cleanse and make clean sinners like
me. Look deep into my heart, dear God, and know that I love
you. Signed: A Bad Woman"

Margaret thought that some glad day when she was in heaven, she would sing for all eternity of the grace of God. Jesus coming to earth to take her place on the cross. To pay for her sin. He truly rescued me she thought, from John and from a life of sin. All the ways she tried to find happiness. He washed her clean and filled her life with joy. What can you say to a God so great?

Within her thoughts, she was thinking, it's okay if I'm sick. It's okay if I'm to die. I have had some great years. Rosemary, my sweet daughter is happy and safe. She has a wonderful family now. She has forgiven me for my past. Some day she will understand more fully my past life. She could see herself as a caterpillar lying on a leaf small and ugly. Then she rejoiced to think how she was changed into a glorious butterfly. Only a great God could perform such a miracle. Praise His name! Will eternity be long enough to thank Him?

You have just finished reading Margarets story, one in which a life was ruined. You may have experienced many emotions, of one kind or another. Perhaps you could have felt, disgust or maybe sympathy. In many ways one person's choices affect another's life. Circumstances have a far reaching way of touching one another and affecting their course in life. I, being the daughter in this story, would like to take you yet a little further into the life of my Mother. "Do you think you are ready for this journey?"

My sweet mother had been in the hospital for about two weeks. In the few years she had lived near my family, she had made many friends. People just seemed to be drawn to her. I thing perhaps, it was her smile, or maybe the gentleness that she showed.

Even as she lay in bed, so very ill, she still helped others with her strong faith and attitude. Margaret had so many visitors. Last night when I visited her, she looked weak but she wanted me to go home and be with my own family.

At home, I could think of nothing else but her Mother. I couldn't go to sleep just yet. I sat down at the kitchen table and picked up my pen...I to found, that I also had a need to pour out my feelings on paper. So I wrote a love poem to my mother.

My Mother, My Friend
How can I let you go, Mother?
So helpless you lie.
No answers from doctors
Nothing money can buy
But how can I turn you loose?
How can I let you go?
I'm fearful, I'm sad and I hurt.
I love you and would do anything
to help you.
If you could look into my heart,
you would see love.
From earliest memories,
it was you I ran to when I was hurt.
When I fell down you dried my tears.
When frightened you calmed my fears.
It was your face I searched for in a crowd
when I needed you.
To you I came for understanding and direction.
The years have come and gone
but you will always be in my heart.

Yes, Mother, wiper of my tears, I love you.
You were the velvet soft and beautiful
that lined my life.

The ringing of the phone wrangled Rosemary's nerves. It was that phone call you dreaded, the one you knew was coming and you didn't want to answer. The nurse said, "You'd better come right away to the hospital."

Rosemary was in a panic. She could hardly button her dress or put her shoes on her feet. She knew that she must hurry to get there. It was evident in the tone of the nurse's voice. She didn't know how she even drove the car. Finally, running down the hallway to her room, she suddenly stopped in the door way of her room and noticed the noise of the oxygen machine had been turned off. There she lay in silence ever so quietly and peaceful.

As she ran over to the bed, she cried, "Look, Mother's reaching out to touch my hand." Then Rosemary knew, she was gone. She sank slowly to the floor and was in tears. Then, although she knew her Mother was gone, it was as if the whole room was suddenly filled with peace. A look of rest on her mothers face seemed to have replaced the years of suffering. It was finally, over. There would be no more pain and no need for the oxygen.

What a life she had lived. No matter what, Rosemary knew, her Mother had given her all of her love, heart and soul.

After saying goodbye to her Mother for the last time, she stepped out into the bright sunshine of a new day. The sky was Easter egg blue. That's when she noticed a bright orange monarch butterfly on a red rose bush. It caught her eye as it soared off into the air. How her mother had loved butterflies, because of the new life they represented. For she believed that God had given her a beautiful new life changing her from an ugly caterpillar into a butterfly. He had certainly made her beautiful to Rosemary and her family . God had touched her life and all of those around her.

As Rosemary wiped the tears away ,that kept running down her face, she smiled and said, "Yes, mother, you will be truly missed." Rosemary spent the rest of that day being close to her own children. Her husband had made all the funeral arrangements for her Mother six months earlier. We all seemed that day, to need to just hold onto each other. We were happy that she was free from sickness, yet sad for the loss of her in our lives. I being, her only child wanted to write a tribute to my mother as we would say goodbye to her. We had all began to call her granny, This made her laugh.

I Remember Granny

How white her hair looked, how blue the color of her eyes.
The sound of her laughter filled the room.
Granny was soft to touch and round to hug.
Money was slipped to each one of her family.
From time to time she took great pleasure
In this gift on the sly.
The little child in her loved to get presents
and she enjoyed giving them to others.
Getting together with family, was the joy of her life.
Going to church was her heart's desire.
Talking about the angel that appeared one night
would make her face light up.
How large it loomed in her room.
How beautiful it looked, all aglow...
and suddenly it was gone!
Many hours were spent reading her Bible;
much time was spent in prayer.
Lonely hours with God as her only friend,

increased her faith, as it grew stronger
and stronger.
God never let her down as person after person
was sent to comfort and meet all her needs.
People loved Grandma: doctors, nurses, waitresses,
friends, neighbors and most of all her family.
Her jolly attitude caused people to enjoy her company.
Many lives were touched and blessed by meeting her.
If I were to sum it up in one memory,
it would be Grandma singing "Oh How I Love Jesus."
The last month of her life, as she suffered
her body wasting away,
She held onto her great faith in her great God!
Moments after death, and her body still warm,
she had a peaceful glow on her face.
" Yes, I Remember Grandma, and I'll
join hundreds whose lives were enriched by this dear lady.

Rosemary Ling

47
the letter

Early the next day Rosemary drove to her Mother's apartment. They had discussed her desire for all of her clothes and belongings to be donated to a homeless shelter after she was gone. The silence of her little place surrounded Rosemary. She could almost sense her presence. This had become a haven of rest and solitude for Margaret in her last years. Her spirit was gone; to be forever with her Lord ,and for that Rosemary was grateful. As Rosemary was cleaning out her dresser next to her bed she saw the red diary. This was the one her Mother had told her about. The very one she was to read after her death. Her hands trembled as she picked it up. She clasped it to her chest "Mother, why did you want me to wait? I will need time ,to get over some of the pain of losing you, before I read these words, from you to me.

Sitting down and holding the dear diary of my mother close to my breast.

Her words written in this diary, from her heart to me. Out of her depths of dispair she had penned these

217

words. To allow me to look deep in to her true feelings for me, her only daughter, while we were separated those many years

My eyes falling up on the page dear diary it begins .... when the last page is read I have feelings too deep to express, it would take time to digest all of her love shown within these pages.........I now must gather all of the clothing and dresses and belongings to be given to the salvation army. The personal mementos were in a small box to be gone through a future time. I will place these in my car. Finally the sweet place ,where mother had found such joy was cleaned out, time to leave and donate to the needy her belongings. The nice lady at the drop off door was pleased to take the bags of clothing and goods .I knew mother would be pleased also as she had made me promise to do this act of kindness for her she always loved to bless others.

****

She wondered as she sat down on the sofa. Opening to the first page she began to read. . .

Dearest Daughter,

I know if you are reading my diary, I'm no longer with you. Please don't weep for me. My life has been so very good. You and your family have been a wonderful blessing. Many times I have wanted to express my deepest feelings to you but couldn't find the right words.

Rosemary had to close the diary many times because the tears filled her eyes and she couldn't read her wonderful, heartfelt words. She placed her Mother's diary into her purse to read another time. She could feel her presence all around, even among the clothes she wore. The few pictures and dishes, were about all of her few belongings. After dropping everything off at the Salvation Army, Rosemary started to drive home when she remembered something very special her Mother had asked her to do for her as she was leaving the hospital one night. She held Rosemary's hand while looking deep into her eyes and she whispered to her, "Please dear, it is very important to me ,after I am gone, that you look in my closet on the top shelf in the very back. In my old brown purse there is a zippered pocket. You will find a letter. Oh no, Rosemary thought as she put the brakes on in the car. In her haste to give her mother,s things away, she had forgotten her Mother's words to her from that night. She had given away that old brown purse. Oh, no, Please God, help me.

Frantically, Rosemary rushed back to the Salvation Army drop off station and asked the lady there to please ,help her to get the brown purse back. She explained the circumstances to the woman and she was very reassuring to her, that they would find the purse. Shortly afterwards, they found the old brown purse and Rosemary was so relieved. She reached into the zippered pocket to see if the letter was in there. There it was, just as her Mother had told her it would be. It had Rosemary's name on it and the words, "For your eyes only."

Although Rosemary could hardly contain her curiosity, she decided to wait until she got back to her Mother's room to read it. After all, she thought, this letter contained a secret from my Mother's past that had been kept, from me until now. She had felt that it was important for me to be alone when I read it. The ride back to the room was slow. At least it seemed that way to Rosemary. When she arrived back at the rooming house, she sat on the couch ,once more and took the letter from her purse and opened the sealed envelope.

Rosemary's hands were shaking and she began to wonder what this letter could be? What was so important to her mother?

Dear Rosemary,

It is with deep regret and great sadness that I must reveal this secret to you. Once more, I must disappoint the one that I love the most you. I will go to my grave with this secret, but I also feel the need to clear my conscience, with you and before I face my God. One night when you were very young, I would say about age fourteen, you were sleeping.

I quietly got out of our bed, trying not to disturb you. I needed to go down the hallway to use the bathroom. A lot of people had sleeping rooms there. We had one upstairs on the third floor. I tried to be quiet not to wake you, as I needed to go down the hallway to the bathroom. Suddenly, when I returned, I noticed that our bedroom door was ajar. As I stepped into the room, a man in dark clothing was getting into your bed, with his pants pulled down, touching you. I could smell the liquor on him. That's when I went crazy I guess. I grabbed an iron pot and pounded him, several times over the head. He fell to the floor. I don't know how I got the super human strength but I dragged him down the hallway and throwing him down the stairway into the stairwell. No one was around or heard him fall. You didn't even wake up. I lay awake all night waiting for someone to come and take me to jail. I had made plans to take you to my Mother's so you could have a better life. I needed to protect you from the streets. While I was in prison.

After awhile, someone found the man, he was dead. He was taken away and the police ruled, it as an accident because he was a known drunkard. The head injury they felt was from the fall all the way down three flights of stairs. I knew differently, I have lived all these many years with this guilt on my soul.

NOW you know, that with all my other sins, you must also, know that I was a murderer too. God forgive me, I would do it all over again, if I needed my darling, to save you. Can you please forgive me? May God have mercy on me. This letter is for your eyes only.

Rosemary fell down on the sofa and sobbed. My dear mother, she thought, how my heart breaks, when I realize that all these years you have lived with this terrible dark secret. How could you bear this burden all alone? Because of me, you sacrificed yourself. You lived in a different kind of hell than the one you lived in with that man, John. No wonder you couldn't sleep. She thought, you never were the real cause of his death. Now you are gone. You are in heaven. Jesus has forgiven you, sweet Mother.

Rosemary only wished she could have had one more chance to thank her once more for her great love and sacrifice for her.

While walking to the sink Rosemary struck a match to the pages of the letter placing them into the sink to burn. The smoke rose up from the ashes, forever sealing this deep dark secret. For the very last time, Rosemary turned the key in the lock and closed the door of the apartment. She walked out into the night. No one must ever know of that terrible secret.

48
saying goodbye

After a brief service at their church, there were many friends offering their sympathy and condolences. My mother would have been proud to see the turnout for her funeral service. People seemed to love her, even though they had only known her for a brief time. She had such a way about her that people became close to her in a short time. I just wanted to be alone to ponder my own feelings and sort out things in her own heart. I also wanted to read every word of my mother's diary, but I knew it would take a few weeks to pull myself together to be able to absorb all of the things that my mother had wanted to share with me.

"Is Granny in heaven?" The children asked once more. "Yes dear." Rosemary answers them once more. "We miss her"they say. "Yes, but she is no longer sick. She is at rest." Rosemary hugs the children close to her. Someday she thinks they may want to read her mothers diary and poetry.

Poem number one.

Little   Fountain

As I look out my window, the world looks quiet apart from me.
Houses have lights in their windows.
Strangers unknown to me live within.
They do not know that I exist. I look at the tree
Outside my window. It looks as though it is doing nothing.
Cars pass and the tree is unobserved but is quietly occupying
The spot where it was planted.
Then I cry but what about me…God?
Here I am alone struggling, not sure of what I am to be.
What is my purpose? Then I hear that still small voice
within me saying Oh my child, my little one, why do you worry
and fret so? Can you not even yet trust me? I am your Father,
the Creator of the universe. You are to be a little fountain of
joy, bubbling and running over with happiness and peace.
That is your purpose! To allow the good things of God to come
forth from you! That's all! Trust me. Rest in my care. Allow
the people of this world to see me in you. So yield yourself to
me once again, and let me fill you to overflowing "Little
Fountain." Then bubble, bubble with joy for all to see! Let
your smile be radiant and laughter be in your mouth as sweet
as honeycomb. Peace shall encompass your being. I shall be
your guide, Yes! I the Fountain Head shall pour forth into your
innermost being, then you will be the source in which I flood,
the world, your world with my joy. As you go through each
hour, each task let me flow. As you work and greet people, I
will flow washing and refreshing the spirits of men as the
streams flow in the desert. I will flow forth from you!
My little Fountain.

Poem number two

Seasons of Love

This is the season of fall.
I look out the window and I see the rain
gently washing the trees and the houses.
The rain makes the air smell so fresh.
The leaves flutter in the wind.
They have covered the ground with
bright orange mixed with gold and red.
My eyes move to the sky and my heart skips a beat.
How beautiful the world looks in fall.

A chill moves through the air
and I know winter is coming fast.
I wait for winter like a dear friend.
I am so thrilled when I see the sprinkling of snow.
Ever so softly painting the world white.
White means purity to me.
Then I think of the Christ child who was born on a night
When snow wrapped the world in white.
As we walk in the crisp air of winter, our cheeks are red,
our eyes sparkle.
My Lord, now I know winter is the best season!

One morning we awake and realize the world is changing.
Could it be spring? Sweet, sweet spring, only now do
I remember how I love her.
I begin to think of birds caring for their young.
I see a small patch of grass and I know
that a wonderful awakening is going on all around.
New life is appearing.
I wait impatiently for the buds that promise a flower.
I love thee, Oh Lord for I feel spring must be

the very best season.

I begin to long for summer.
I want more and more of the warmth of the sun.
I yearn to be engulfed in the beauty of sunshine.
The grass is clothed in green.
The trees are so full of life, they seem to be
forever stretching upward toward the sun.
Summer is a peaceful season.
We can walk in the sunshine and smell the air
so full of the scent of flowers.
I long to be near you, my Father, in the summer
and pass slowly through the seasons.

Each one seems so dear, each one so beautiful.
Then, I begin to realize why I love the seasons.
It is because of you, oh God.
With you beside me, the world can never be
anything but beautiful.
Oh wondrous God, how you must love us
to show thyself in nature.

#######diary?

Two years have passed.

Rosemary remembers back to that time when her Mother passed, she was a younger woman then with a young family and now she is the older one. The years have passed swiftly. Rosemary still felt empty and alone so she visited her Mother's grave today. She had been laid to rest in a quiet graveyard. An old oak tree is shedding its leaves and they fall upon the ground so softly. There are different colors of red and gold and yellow. Rosemary needed to spent some time at the grave site.

wanted a few moments of solitude. My Mother is at rest
, she thought. She had suffered for so many years and
in so many ways while she lived here on Earth. She had
never once complained to Rosemary about her past life.
Approaching the grave, she notices a tall dark silhouette
standing over her mothers grave. He appears to be crying.
He slowly stooped to the ground and placed a single red
rose bud on her grave. Speaking to my mother he said,
'My dearest love, I have come too late_ please forgive me.
I have always loved you.'
   Rosemary, is shocked, and walking closer to the
grave site, the leaves rustle under her feed. Startled,
the weeping stranger stood up quickly and looked into
Rosemary,s eyes.'You must be Margaret,s beautiful
daughter, Rosemary,' Remembering the face in the gold
heart shaped locket, she was speechless. 'How do you
know my mother?.' 'My name is Howard Jones, we were
to be married. I should have been your Father; however,
I made a foolish mistake while severing overseas , and
married the wrong women. Your mother was my soul
mate, and I will go to my grave loving her, but I came too
late!' ' I searched for her ,for years, but came to find her
too late.' When Rosemary looked into Howard,s eyes, she
knew that he had spoken from his heart. That's when she
removed the heart shaped locket from around her neck
and showed Howard the two pictures ,one of them was
her, that were inside. Finally, the mystery man had been
unveiled, and she now knew, the man in the other picture
was Howard. Astonished, Howard,s eyes began to fill up
once more with tears, and roll down his cheek. 'Mother
was truly happy in her last years. ' 'She was just a Granny
who loved Jesus.' "Jesus, I Love Thee" was her favorite
hymn. 'In my minds eye ,I can imagine her up in heaven
being with the beautiful angels and her own Mother and
Father.' Rosemary, bows her head and prays, "Please

God, tell my Mother to wait for me and someday, all of us will be joined together in perfect peace. Amen."

That's when they, first noticed it; out of the corner of their eye;s . It flit upon a red flower bud and land ,for just for just a quick second ,and then fly away. It was a beautiful yellow Monarch butterfly. It seemed to be a sign of new life and new hope given to them. It was at that moment, from her mother ,a message ,that seemed to say to them ,the two loves of her life, had finally met ,and she was happy and could rest in peace.

It was also a sign given to Howard , that he had found forgiveness .from her Mother. As Rosemary , said 'goodbye to Howard ,and she would keep in touch with him. She returned to her car, there was a sprinkle of soft rain drops, as though they were sharing, together in tears a time, or refreshing, for this brief moment. Through her tears, Rosemary was able to smile just a bit, as she had found a perfect peace within.

Soon, she would be home once more, surrounded by her loved ones. Life was really good for her now. The words from the song, "Jesus, I Love Thee" came to mind as the night softly closed in on her. Sleep well my mother, sleep well.

Did you like what you read?
Ask me about this and my other books
Rosemary Ling, author
(239)543-3858

23699502R00134

Made in the USA
Charleston, SC
02 November 2013